Changeling Press LLC
ChangelingPress.com

Cheshire (Underland MC 2)
A Bad Boys MC Romance
Harley Wylde

Cheshire (Underland MC 2)
A Bad Boys MC Romance
Harley Wylde

ISBN: 978-1-60521-932-5

Publisher:
Changeling Press LLC
315 N. Centre St.
Martinsburg, WV 25404
ChangelingPress.com

Printed in the U.S.A.

Editor: Crystal Esau
Cover Artist: Bryan Keller

The individual stories in this anthology have been previously released in E-Book format.

Table of Contents

Cheshire (Underland MC 2)
A Bad Boys MC Romance
Harley Wylde

Cheshire is perfect for fans of suspense and forbidden love stories.

Eliza -- Being the daughter of the sheriff might sound nice to most people. But they don't know what my father is truly like. All they see is the mask he wears. The congenial smile, the good deeds, and the way he puts others before himself. It's all an act. Behind closed doors, he's a monster. One I can't seem to escape. Until I've finally had enough... my daring attempt to leave home lands me in the arms of the VP of the Underland MC... and something tells me there's no safer place to be.

Cheshire -- As the VP of the Underland MC, and former military, I'm no stranger to dangerous situations. When my club discovers the local sheriff is corrupting the town of Warren, I know we need to step in. Human trafficking and abuse are just the tip of the iceberg when it comes to the sheriff and his henchmen. But the one thing I never expected to find was love -- especially with the sheriff's innocent daughter. I'll make sure to take the bastard down, not only for the town of Warren, but for Eliza. I never want to see fear in her eyes again.

Are you ready for this gripping tale of danger and desire?

Chapter One
Eliza

The room swam in a haze of fear and broken glass. Sheriff Holmes' face twisted into an ugly snarl, eyes burning with rage. He clenched his fists, knuckles turning white. This wasn't anything new for my father. Just another day in my miserable life.

"Stand up," he barked, voice like ice. I forced myself to my feet, trembling like a leaf, tears streaming down my face.

"Please don't," I whispered, but my words fell on deaf ears.

"Shut up!" His fist collided with my cheekbone, the force sending me sprawling back to the floor. The air rushed from my lungs as if I'd been sucker punched. Pain exploded through my skull.

This is it. This is how I die.

"Get up," he spat again, reveling in the torment he inflicted. The darkness in his eyes chilled me to the core. I scrambled to my feet, legs shaking, praying for some kind of reprieve.

"Look at you," he sneered, grabbing a fistful of my hair and yanking me closer. "Pathetic."

"Please, stop," I whimpered, too weak to resist his iron grip. In that moment, I knew I was nothing to him -- just another thing to control and bend to his will. He'd never think of me as a daughter, as family. I wasn't sure a monster like him was capable of such a thing.

"Did you think I'd let you get away with it? That I wouldn't find out?" He punctuated his words with a vicious blow to my stomach, causing bile to rise in my throat.

Can't breathe. Can't fight back. Just need to survive. I

curled up to protect my already battered body.

"Learn your place," he hissed as he landed one final punch, then turned to leave, his heavy footsteps echoing in my ears.

I didn't know what I'd done to make him so angry this time. It could have been anything. Maybe I'd put something in the wrong place. I didn't think I'd ruined any of his clothes when I'd done the laundry. No matter how hard I thought about it, I had no idea what I'd done.

Blood dripped down my face, each droplet a painful reminder of the violent flurry that had just unfolded. I stared at the cracked mirror on the wall, catching glimpses of my battered reflection between the jagged lines. The pain was unbearable, but what hurt more was the feeling of utter helplessness.

"Is this it?" I whispered to myself, choking back tears. "Is this all my life will ever be?"

My eyes scanned the room, taking in the shattered glass and twisted remnants of what had once been my sanctuary. How could I ever feel safe again, knowing that he'd violated every inch of this space?

I pressed my hand against my bruised ribs, wincing at the sharp stab of pain. For a moment, I allowed myself to imagine a world where the torture ceased, where I could finally be free from his sadistic grip.

"Maybe death would be better," I admitted, my voice barely audible. "At least then, I wouldn't have to live in fear."

The thought sent shivers down my spine, but also brought an odd sense of comfort. In death, there would be peace. No more beatings, no more humiliation, no more heart-pounding terror that gripped me every time he approached. Even if there was nothing but a sea of darkness on the other side, it would be preferable to this.

"Eliza," my father's voice cut through my thoughts, and I realized he was standing in my doorway again. "Don't think I'm done with you. If you ever try to defy me again, I won't hesitate to end your miserable existence."

Fear slithered its way into my throat, choking me as I struggled to find my voice. "Yes, sir," I managed to whisper, quivering under the weight of his gaze. I couldn't ask *how* I'd defied him. Doing so would only spark his anger again.

"Remember that." With one last chilling glare, he slammed the door behind him, leaving me to wallow in my own despair.

Trembling, I realized that even the thought of death couldn't save me. The fear of my father, of Sheriff Holmes, held me captive in a prison more terrifying than any physical cage.

"Death or life," I whispered into the void. "Either way, I'm trapped."

My heart pounded, and my hands shook. I didn't even remember my mother anymore. She'd died so long ago. I thought we were happier then, but I didn't know for sure. Had my father always been a monster?

"No escape." If I tried... I dragged myself up, wincing. Bruised, battered, weak. That's what I saw when I looked in the mirror. At times like this, I hated myself. If I were strong, would I be able to stand up to him? Or if I were more cunning, could I escape?

"Damn him," I muttered, the words barely escaping my swollen lips.

The sound of motorcycles roared in the distance. I knew they'd belong to the local motorcycle club. I'd seen them at a distance many times.

A light tap on my window drew me over to it. "Who's there?"

I kept my voice low, not wanting to draw my father's attention again. "It's Maria from next door."

"Maria," I breathed, relief washing over me for a brief moment. We weren't exactly close, but she'd noticed my wounds before and done her best to help. Although she too feared my father.

"Open the window," she urged.

"Can't be seen together," I reminded her, my gaze darting around the room in panic. "He'll hurt us both. If he thinks you're helping me…"

"Eliza, listen," she said urgently. "I've found help. The Underland MC. I think if you can get to them, they'll protect you."

"Protect me?" I scoffed, disbelief coloring my tone. "From Sheriff Holmes? No one can do that. It would be different if my father were anyone else."

"They can," Maria insisted. "Those men aren't scared of anyone. I don't have proof, but I think they're responsible for something big that went down a few weeks ago."

"Help from bikers?" I questioned, my mind racing. "How can I trust them?"

"They look big and scary, but they do a lot of good around town. And from what I've heard, they're all ex-military," she said. "They're your only shot, Eliza."

"All right, but how?" I asked.

"Tonight. If you can get away, I can take you to them. I was behind one of them at the grocery store earlier. Heard him on the phone talking about meeting everyone at a diner in town."

"I'll try." I didn't want to think of the consequences if my father caught me. He might actually kill me.

* * *

I'd waited until I heard my father leave the house, and night had fallen. Then I'd slowly opened my bedroom door and crept down the hall. I'd made it all the way to the front door when someone grabbed my hair and yanked me off my feet.

I yelped and dropped to the floor as they released me. When I looked up, my heart raced. My father, Sheriff Holmes, towered over me. His cold eyes seemed to pierce through my soul, a cruel smile dancing on his lips.

"Think you're clever, huh?" he sneered, hatred dripping from his words. "Where were you slinking off to?"

I tried to shrink back, but the wall left me no escape. Fear clawed at my insides, and I instinctively raised my hands in a feeble attempt to protect myself.

"Please," I whispered, tears streaming down my face.

He lunged forward, his fist connecting with my jaw. Pain exploded through my skull, making my vision blur.

"Pathetic," he spat, grabbing me by the hair and yanking me up.

"Stop!" I cried out, frantically trying to pull away from his grip.

"Or what?" he taunted, his voice cold and ruthless. "You gonna cry for Mommy? Oh, wait... She's dead."

He struck my ribs repeatedly, until I thought I might die. The pain was unbearable, taking over every inch of my body. My breath came in ragged gasps, each one feeling like a knife in my chest.

"Please," I choked out again, my voice barely

audible. "No more."

"Are you gonna learn your lesson now?" he asked, his tone mocking.

"Y-yes," I stammered, terror forcing me to submit.

"Good," he growled, finally releasing his grip on my hair. He let me crumple to the floor, my battered body screaming in agony.

"Remember this," he said, his voice menacingly low. "You ever try to defy me again, and it'll be the last thing you ever do."

"Understood," I whispered, tears streaming down my bruised and swollen face.

"Pathetic," he muttered one last time before stalking out of the house, leaving me a broken mess on the floor.

After he left, I lay there for a while, pain radiating from every inch of me. But I couldn't give up. Not now. Slowly, painstakingly, I pushed myself up from the floor, my body protesting against the movement.

"Dad's gone," I whispered to myself, a feeble attempt at bolstering my courage. Leaning against the wall for support, I stumbled toward the front door.

My hands shook as I reached out for the knob, biting down hard on my lip to stifle a cry of pain. Pulling it open was torture. Every fiber in my being screamed in protest.

Once outside, the chilly night air hit my face like a slap. It stung and soothed in equal measure against my battered skin. Tears filled my eyes and for a moment, everything blurred. Blinking them away, I forced myself to focus. There was no room for mistakes.

The next few steps were agonizing and

seemingly impossible. Each one felt like walking through a field of broken glass.

I had almost reached Maria's house when the roar of engines filled the air. Panic surged through me. I pressed myself against the shadowy side of a nearby shed to hide.

Moments later, several motorcycles roared past me on the main road, their riders hidden behind darkened helmets. My heart pounded in my chest as they zoomed by. Were these the men Maria had told me about? No. They didn't wear the black leather vests like the others did.

After they had passed and silence returned to our quiet neighborhood, I pushed myself upright again and limped toward Maria's house.

Just as I reached her door, it swung open, and she stepped out into her yard. Her eyes widened when she saw me in the moonlight.

"Oh, God," she gasped, rushing toward me with hurried steps.

"I tried," was all I managed to mutter before my legs gave way beneath me and I fell into her arms, the world spinning in a whirlwind of excruciating pain and darkness.

Maria caught me before I hit the ground, her small frame straining under my weight. She muttered something under her breath as she struggled to keep us both upright, her eyes aflame with determination and worry.

"We're going to get you out of here, Eliza," she said fiercely, her voice barely above a whisper. But I wasn't sure if I believed her anymore. The pain was too much, the situation too dire. My father's threats echoed in my ears.

As unconsciousness loomed, my last thought

was that I wouldn't survive this hell much longer.

My weak body gave up completely then, and I sank into darkness, any fight left in me evaporating.

* * *

When I came to, Maria was doing her best to clean my wounds, her face a mask of focused concentration. "You're going to be okay," she kept repeating, more for herself than for me.

I knew she was lying, but I didn't have the strength to argue. Instead, I let her work in silence, my body throbbing with pain. With each swab of disinfectant she applied, a new wave of agony washed over me, causing me to grit my teeth against the discomfort.

"How long was I out?" I asked.

"Nearly twenty minutes," she murmured.

Suddenly, the sound of an approaching car made us freeze. It stopped nearby, and somehow, I just knew it was my father. I heard our door slam shut, then his bellow of rage.

"It's him," Maria whispered to me. She looked pale under the dim light pouring in from the lone window. In that moment, I knew we were thinking the same thing -- we were trapped.

But Maria was not one to give up easily. She quickly helped me into a small cupboard near the window, covering me with blankets before closing the door as quietly as possible.

"You need to be quiet," she instructed, her voice barely audible.

I nodded from behind the door and watched through a crack as she ran into the darkness toward the backdoor.

"Maria!" my father bellowed loudly enough for the whole neighborhood to hear.

I peeked through a crack in the door and watched as he barged into Maria's house with his men following closely behind. Deputies just as twisted as my father. They'd do anything for him. They roughly tore through every room searching for me while Maria desperately tried to convince them that I wasn't there.

Tears welled up in my eyes as he held Maria against a wall, my father's face inches from hers.

"Where is she?" he threatened, gripping Maria by the throat.

Maria managed to choke out a defiant response, "She's gone... You'll never find her."

I watched in horror as my father's fist connected with Maria's face, sending her sprawling onto the floor. His men joined in, their cruel laughter echoing off the walls.

Anger boiled within me, but I was helpless. They continued to torment Maria while I hid. I heard every punch, every kick, every blow. I wanted to scream, to fight back, but I couldn't. All I could do was curl up inside the cupboard and pray for it to be over.

As dawn approached, they finally left. Silence hung heavy in the air once they were gone.

Shaky and weak, I pushed the cupboard door open and stumbled over to where Maria lay motionless on the floor.

"Maria," I choked out, gently shaking her. She groaned in pain but didn't open her eyes.

"I'm so sorry," I sobbed as guilt washed over me. This was all my fault. All this pain and suffering was because of my inability to stand up to my father.

But as tears streamed down my cheeks, something deep within me stirred -- a spark of determination that hadn't been there before.

I wouldn't let him win.

Maria needed help, but who could I call? My hand shook as I reached for her phone and pulled up the number for one of her family members. They didn't answer so I left a message. Until someone arrived, I'd wait with her, and do what I could. Getting up, I went to fetch warm, damp towels to clean her up. Maybe the damage wasn't as bad as I feared.

Why do I have to be so useless?

Chapter Two

Cheshire

The sound of leather creaking and boots shuffling filled the air as Hatter's voice rang out, steady and authoritative. "Everyone listen up!"

I stood near the back, watching as the room settled into a hushed silence, every pair of eyes locked on our president. The weight of the moment hung heavy, but Hatter wore it like a well-tailored suit.

"First order of business," he continued, not wasting any time. His words were sharp and clear, slicing through the tension like a razor blade. It was that same commanding tone that had gotten us through more scrapes than I could count.

"Rabbit, Carpenter, March -- you've got that run to Ironwood coming up. But I have a feeling we'll be postponing it." He eyed each of them. "Next, we need to address the situation with Sheriff Holmes."

That name sent a ripple of anger through the crowd, like a match tossed into a pool of gasoline. During our recent ordeal with Eddie Lewis, we'd discovered just how deep the corruption ran in our town.

"Cheshire's got something for us on that front." Hatter turned to me, his eyes narrowed in anticipation.

"Damn right, I do," I muttered under my breath. Everyone focused on me, their loyalty burning hotter than hellfire. This wasn't just about taking down a corrupt sheriff -- it was about protecting our town, our people. And nobody messed with Underland MC.

"Then let's hear it," Hatter commanded, gesturing for me to step forward.

As I moved toward the center of the room, I felt the unyielding strength of the brotherhood behind me.

United by blood, sweat, and chrome, we were a force to be reckoned with. And together, we'd bring that bastard Holmes to his knees.

"All right," I began, taking a deep breath. "Here's what we're going to do… We gather evidence against that son of a bitch. We expose his dirty deeds. We make sure everyone in Warren knows what kind of monster they've got wearing a badge."

I could feel the weight of their attention on me, their trust a hot brand searing into my skin. But I knew what had to be done, and I'd do whatever it took to finish what we'd started.

"Rabbit, March, and Carpenter… I have some key jobs for you. I'll give you the details in a minute."

"Got it, Cheshire," Rabbit replied, his voice steady as he nodded in agreement. The others echoed his sentiment, their determination burning bright in their eyes.

As I looked around the room, I knew we were more than just a bunch of bikers. We were family, bound by blood and loyalty. And together, we'd tear down the corruption that had infected our home.

"Remember, boys," I warned, my voice low and deadly, "this won't be easy. Holmes won't go down without a fight. But we've got something he doesn't -- the power of brotherhood. It's going to take all of us to see this through."

"Damn straight," Hatter chimed in, his gravelly voice bolstering our resolve. "We're with you all the way, Cheshire."

"Then let's get to work," I said, clenching my fist in determination. "For Underland MC. For Warren. And for every single person that bastard has hurt."

"*Underland*!" the club roared as one, their voices shaking the very foundations of the clubhouse.

Together, we'd bring justice to this town. United, we'd make damn sure Sheriff Daniel Holmes paid for his sins. No one messed with the Underland MC, or with our town.

"Got any intel on where we can find some solid evidence?" Rabbit asked, his voice anxious but steady. His gaze darted around the room, taking in every detail like he always did -- constantly calculating.

"Been working on that," I said, tapping my temple with a smirk. "Got a couple leads I'm looking into, and I'm sure our corrupt sheriff has left a trail we can follow." My mind raced through the possibilities, planning and plotting each step with precision.

Carpenter grunted, his massive frame nearly dwarfing the others. "Just say the word, brother. We'll be there when it's time to throw down."

My gaze swept across the room one last time, feeling the pulse of determination that connected us all. This was more than just a war on corruption -- this was personal. For Underland MC, for Warren, and for every soul that had been hurt by Sheriff Holmes' twisted games.

"All right, then," I said, clapping my hands together. "Let's get to work. And remember, we got each other's backs. No one goes in alone."

As we dispersed, I couldn't help but feel a mix of anticipation and dread. This was going to be one hell of a fight, but together, we'd see it through to the end. Nothing would stand in our way.

A select few stayed behind and we claimed a table. Hatter leaned back in his chair, arms folded, clearly leaving me to do the talking.

My fingers tapped against the table, itching to get shit done. Glancing around at my brothers, their eyes locked on me, I knew we were all on the same page.

"All right, listen up," I said, my voice low and gravelly. "Each of you has a part to play in this. We're going to hit Holmes where it hurts."

Rabbit whipped out a notepad, eyes wide and focused as he scribbled down every word that left my mouth. His brow furrowed, deep in concentration, making sure no detail escaped him. It was almost amusing how his hand shook ever so slightly as he wrote -- Rabbit's nervous energy made him perfect for the job.

"March, we'll need you to use your computer skills to find out any weaknesses we can exploit." I watched March nod, his face hardening with resolve.

"Rabbit, you'll be coordinating intel. Keep track of everything we learn, make sure it's secure. You know what to do." Rabbit nodded fervently, already organizing his notes into neat little bullet points. His dedication never wavered, even when the stakes were high.

As I laid out the rest of the assignments, my brothers continued to listen intently, nodding along as they soaked up the details. Trust flowed through us like blood, thick and unwavering. These men were my family, and together we'd face whatever hell awaited us.

"Carpenter," I continued, turning to face the mountain of a man on my right. He sat, tense as a coiled spring, his stern gaze never leaving mine. "You're going to be our main line of defense if things go south. We're going to need your strength more than ever."

Carpenter grunted, his eyes glinting with unspoken fury under the dim lights of the clubhouse. "Just give me a time and place."

I smiled at his determination, feeling a surge of pride for my brothers. We all knew what we'd signed up for when we founded Underland MC, and none of us were about to back down now.

"Hatter," I finally said, turning to the president of our club. His eyes held an intensity that was steadfast, commanding respect without demanding it. "Keep your eyes on the bigger picture. You're our leader and we trust your judgment above all else."

Hatter nodded solemnly, understanding the weight of his role within our family. "We'll get this bastard," he affirmed, his voice resolute.

With each directive given, every member in our little circle understood their part in this dangerous mission. The atmosphere crackled with anticipation and resolve as the clock ticked away in the unnerving silence. Each of us lost in our thoughts, planning for the impending storm.

"We're not just taking on Holmes," I reminded them, my voice turning bitter. "We're taking on every corrupt shit who's ever crossed us or our town."

The room darkened as shadows played across the rugged faces of my brothers -- men forged in adversity yet bound by loyalty. A silent pledge passing through each one of us, to take down Holmes and anyone who stood with him.

"Let's get some sleep," Hatter commanded after a few moments of silence, breaking the tension in the room. "We need to be sharp for what's coming."

The ensuing chaos of dragging chairs and grunts of agreement broke the hush as we each rose to our feet. I watched my brothers disband and head toward their respective quarters, a silent camaraderie between us.

Turning off the last light in the clubhouse, I

mulled over the events of this fateful meeting. I knew the upcoming battle would be tough, every bit as treacherous as any we'd seen before. Yet something in my gut told me this was it -- our chance to rid Warren of corruption and make it a place we could take pride in again.

As I settled into my bed, the faces of my brothers flashed through my mind like a reel. Their loyalty and faith in one another were our greatest weapons against Holmes' corrupt reign. No matter what happened next, we would stand firm, side by side in the face of adversity.

I closed my eyes, letting the silence envelop me.

Tomorrow would bring a new dawn... A dawn where either we stood victorious or perished trying. But one thing was certain: we wouldn't go down without a fight. No matter how long it took, I'd make sure that man never hurt anyone again.

* * *

It felt like I'd barely fallen asleep when the first rays of the sun hit my tired eyes. My nerves were humming with anticipation and adrenaline. Getting out of bed, I took a minute to organize my scattered thoughts.

Striding into the kitchen, I saw Rabbit already at work, his notes spread out on the table in front of him. His concentration broke only for a moment as he looked up, giving me a small nod before going back to his work. His constant state of worry was part of what made him so damn good at his job.

I found Carpenter next, his hulking frame leaned over the weight bench in our makeshift gym. Sweat rolled down his face as he grunted, pushing up another heavy rep. His commitment to strength and protection never ceased to amaze me.

Stepping outside into the yard, I found March standing there with his arms crossed over his chest, foot tapping against the gravel. The cool morning breeze brushed against us as March's stern gaze bored into me. Although he didn't say much, his eyes said everything -- he was ready for battle.

Lastly, I found Hatter in his office, hunched over maps and blueprints scattered across the desk. He looked up as I walked in and gave me a firm nod. As president of Underland MC, Hatter carried our trust on his shoulders every day. Today was no different.

I left all of them to their tasks and guzzled a few cups of coffee. I hadn't seen Jo this morning, and I wondered if she was sleeping in. The fact I'd pulled Hatter from his bed so early probably irked her, but if she knew why, she'd understand.

An hour later, we all gathered in the kitchen. "Got everything you need?"

Everyone nodded in response while they busied themselves preparing for what lay ahead -- checking weapons, gathering equipment, going through checklists Rabbit had meticulously prepared.

There was a certain electricity in the air as we moved around each other in practiced silence -- each man knowing exactly what needed to be done. As I watched my brothers prepare for our fight against Holmes and his corrupt system, I couldn't help but feel a surge of pride.

We all knew the risks. We understood that our actions might lead to severe consequences. But we also knew that we had a shot at changing Warren, at ridding it of its poisoned roots, and no amount of danger would keep us from trying.

"Remember," I said, breaking the silence as we prepared to head out. "This isn't just about taking down Holmes. This is about making a difference to our town. To our home."

The room filled with a tense silence as my words hung in the air before March broke it, his voice gruff and determined, "Let's get to work, then."

Riding out toward the day of reckoning ahead, I could feel the determination radiating from each member of Underland MC. We were more than just a motorcycle club. We were brothers united by a common cause. Our loyalty had been forged in battle long before there had ever been an Underland MC.

As the roar of our bikes echoed through Warren's early morning stillness, I knew this was only the beginning. As long as Holmes and his kind threatened what we held dear, we'd stand against them.

We weren't just defending ourselves. We were defending Warren and its people. Because when you're part of Underland MC -- when you're part of this family -- you don't back down. You fight for what's right. And if today was any indication, we were ready for one hell of a fight.

We wouldn't bring Sheriff Holmes to his knees today, but we'd start laying the foundation. Soon, he'd pay the price for all he'd done.

Chapter Three

Eliza

I winced, pain shooting through my face as my fingers brushed against the bruises. Damn, he really let loose on me this time. Dad's fists were no joke. I could feel the anger bubbling inside me, but I knew it was pointless. He was the sheriff, untouchable. Who was I going to report him to? Everyone in this town thought the man was perfect. The ones who knew of the darker side of him wouldn't help me escape.

"Fuck," I whispered to myself, standing in the dimly lit room that was supposed to be my sanctuary.

My eyes surveyed the aftermath of my father's wrath, taking in the shattered pieces of what were once my things. It wasn't much, but every broken trinket and ripped photo was a reminder of how messed up my life was. I was trapped in this hellhole, and there wasn't a damn thing I could do about it.

"God, I hate him," I muttered under my breath, picking up a shard of glass from my favorite picture frame. The image of Mom and me when I was just a kid, her smiling face all crumpled and torn, made my heart ache.

Keep it together. There has to be a way out of here. But how? How could I escape the monster who had all the power and control?

"Think, Eliza, think," I mumbled to myself, trying to focus on anything other than the pain and fear that were eating me alive. "You're smarter than him. You're stronger than you know."

Except… was I really? If I'd been so smart, why was I still here? It wasn't like I was a child anymore. I could have run. Left town and never looked back. And yet, there'd always been this fear that he'd track me down, drag me back here, and my life would be even worse than it was now.

"Maybe," I admitted to the empty room, glancing around at the wreckage one last time before I curled up on my bed, defeated. "But maybe not today."

For now, I would bide my time, wait for my chance to break free from this nightmare. And when that day came, I swore on Mom's grave, I'd never look back.

The rumble of engines broke through the silence, making me jump. I scrambled to my feet, wincing as my battered body protested. The sound grew louder, and something inside me urged me to take a look.

"Who's out there?" I whispered, inching closer to the window. My heart raced with a mixture of fear and anticipation. Was it the Underland MC, or the same bikers I'd seen before? The ones who weren't part of a club. I had no way of knowing if those other men were just a friendly group who enjoyed riding, or if they were something more.

As I peered through the glass, I saw them -- the Underland MC, riding past in a tight formation. Their leather vests made them look like some sort of army. Each one of them was a towering figure, muscles bulging under their vests. They were nothing like the weak, beaten girl I'd become.

"Damn," I breathed out, my eyes glued to the sight. Hatter, the leader of the pack, caught my eye. He looked like a man who knew pain but somehow had survived it all. If I could beg them for help, would it do me any good?

Who's that? My gaze locked onto one biker in particular. He had this mischievous grin plastered on his face. My heart picked up its pace as I watched him ride past, captivating me in a way I'd never experienced before.

As I watched him, I wondered if he was the one they called Cheshire. Something about this man had me hooked. My stomach twisted into knots as I kept staring, wondering what kind of life he led, if it was anything like the hell I was stuck in right now.

"Eliza!" I heard my father roar from downstairs, pulling me back to reality. "Get your ass down here!"

"Coming, Daddy," I called back, dread churning in my gut. I tore my gaze away from the bikers, wishing I could hop on one of their bikes and ride away from this hell forever.

My thoughts remained on the bikers. Did they have their own code of honor? Or did they protect everyone equally? If I could just reach out to them... in their world, maybe I wouldn't be a victim. I could be strong. Free.

Snap out of it Eliza! Stop dreaming.

"Eliza!" My father's voice boomed again, making me flinch. The bikers, their engines still roaring, began to fade into the distance, leaving me alone with my thoughts.

"Maybe one day," I murmured, clenching my fists as I headed for the door. "One day, I'll find a way out of this mess."

For now, though, I had to face the music. With a heavy heart, I stepped out of my room and descended the stairs, hoping that someday, I wouldn't have to fear what lay beyond my own front door. Or on this side of it either, for that matter.

"Eliza, get down here!" My father's voice echoed through the house. I knew I had to go downstairs, but my mind was still racing, filled with questions about Cheshire and the Underland MC.

Were they happy? Could they -- no *he* -- be my

ticket out of this nightmare?

"So help me God, if your ass isn't down here in the next three seconds, you're going to regret it!" I trembled in fear as I hastened to my father's side. Would I ever find the courage to escape? If I did, would the Underland MC be the key like Maria seemed to think?

* * *

The door slammed shut behind me, blocking out Daddy's growls. My room was a mess, like always, but tonight it felt more suffocating than ever. Pain throbbed in my face as I made my way to the window. I needed something to take my mind off the hurt.

"Damn it," I muttered, clenching my fists so tight my knuckles turned white. "I have to get out of here."

You think you're gonna leave? Daddy's voice echoed through my head, making me shudder. *You ain't going nowhere, girl.*

"Shut up," I whispered, drowning him out with my own voice. "I'll find a way."

Stupid girl, he taunted, and I shook him from my thoughts, focusing on the street outside instead. I watched the empty road, hoping for some distraction -- but there wasn't anything.

"Cheshire," I breathed, remembering the biker who'd ridden past earlier. He had this air about him, like he didn't give a damn about anything. Maybe he could help me... or maybe not. But it was worth a shot.

I knew if I stayed, I'd end up dead. But if I ran... yeah, I could die faster. Once my father caught me, he wouldn't hold back. I'd gotten off easy after going to Maria's. He'd threatened me, beaten the hell out of me, but I was still alive. I'd call that a win for now. Not that it felt like he'd held back at any time, but I knew differently. If he hadn't, I'd have been dead long ago.

Maybe the sheriff couldn't cover up the murder of his own daughter. Not when he was the one to blame. Most people didn't know what he was like, but the ones who did... like Maria... maybe one of them would speak out against him if I died at his hands. At least Maria was safe for now. But if she helped me again...

The sharp sting of pain jolted through me as I shifted on my bed, the bruises from earlier screaming out a cruel reminder. Daddy always knew where to hit so it hurt the most. Lying on my back, I stared up at the cracked ceiling, letting my mind wander back to those leather-clad bikers riding past my window. It felt like they were reaching into my soul and awakening a long-lost hope.

"Maybe there's more for me out there," I whispered, my heart racing at the idea of breaking free from this hellhole. The thought made me shiver with a mix of fear and excitement, but I knew I couldn't just walk out of here without looking back. Not yet, anyway. I had to be smart, patient, and find the right moment to make my move.

I closed my eyes and thought about what my rescue might look like. I'd hear a voice outside my window...

* * *

"Hey, kid," a voice called from below, snatching my attention. "You look like you need a friend."

My heart skipped a beat as I peered down and saw Cheshire standing there, smirking up at me. "What are you doing here?"

"I saw you watching me earlier. Thought I'd come back, see if you needed some help," he replied, his eyes sparkling with mischief. "So, what's the deal? You in trouble or something?"

"Something like that," I admitted, glancing back at my wrecked room. "But there's nothing you can do about it."

"You sure about that?" Cheshire challenged, leaning against his bike. "I've been known to work a few miracles in my time."

"Really?" I asked, skeptically.

"Really." He nodded. "Now, how about you come on down here and tell me what's going on? Maybe we can figure something out together."

"All right... but just give me a second," I whispered, hoping Daddy didn't hear us talking. "I'll be right down."

"Take your time, sweetheart." Cheshire smirked. "I'm not going anywhere."

As I slipped out of my room, my heart raced in anticipation. This was it! I'd finally be free.

* * *

I sighed and stared up at my ceiling. There was no use in dreaming about an escape that might never happen. And the biker from before certainly wasn't going to show up and save me.

I'd have to save myself. It was a daunting thought, but one that I knew was true. No one was coming to rescue me -- no knight in shining armor or biker with a mischievous grin. Only I could pull myself out of this hellhole.

I forced myself up from my bed, wincing at the pain that shot through me. My gaze landed on my mirror, and for a moment, I didn't recognize the girl staring back at me. Bruised, battered, and broken -- I was a ghastly sight. But behind those haunted eyes, I saw something else -- a spark of determination, an ember of hope.

Grimacing from the pain, I started to formulate a

plan. A daring escape into the night, toward freedom and safety... It was a risk, but anything was better than enduring another night of Daddy's wrath. I didn't know if he had people watching the house, if he'd hidden cameras, or anything else. But if I didn't try again, then I'd be stuck in this house, used as his punching bag, until the day I died.

The moonlight crept through the gap in the curtains, casting eerie shadows on the walls. Fatigue pulled at me and I lay back down. My eyelids fluttered closed, and I felt sleep dragging me under, but I fought it for a moment longer. Cheshire's eyes, that mischievous grin, they were all I could see as darkness swallowed me whole.

Even in my dreams, he helped me escape from this miserable life...

* * *

"Eliza," his voice echoed through, smooth as silk, "come with me."

"Where are we going?" I asked, looking around at the strange landscape. Everything was blurry, like a watercolor painting left out in the rain.

"Somewhere better," he answered, a coy smile playing on his lips. "You don't have to live like this anymore."

"Promise?" I whispered, tears prickling at the corners of my eyes. Was this what hope felt like?

"Promise," he said, taking my hand, and the warmth of his touch sent shivers down my spine. We raced through the dream-world together, leaving the pain and fear behind like dust in our wake.

But then, just as we were about to crest a hill, something pulled me back, an invisible chain yanking me away from Cheshire. I reached out, but he was already fading into the distance, his fingers slipping from mine.

"Wait!" I cried, desperation clawing at my throat. "Don't leave me!"

"Find me, Eliza," he called back, his voice growing fainter by the second. "I'll be waiting."

"Cheshire!" I screamed, but it was too late -- he was gone. And all that was left was the aching emptiness inside me, worse than any bruise or broken bone.

* * *

I jolted awake, gasping for air, my heart pounding like a jackhammer in my chest. It was just a dream -- but maybe it was a sign too. Maybe Cheshire really was the key to my freedom, the one who could help me break these chains.

The darkness closed in again, heavy as a shroud, and I let it take me. But even in the blackest depths of night, the image of Cheshire's mischievous grin remained, a glimmer of hope that refused to be snuffed out.

Chapter Four

Cheshire

Hatter had given me the lead on the issue with the sheriff. Which meant I didn't necessarily have to run everything by him. As long as I kept him in the loop, that's all that mattered. From what I'd heard, other clubs didn't run the same way ours did. But since we were all ex-military, and most of us had served together, we were used to working as a team.

We'd found some interesting intel, but it wasn't enough. I needed more details to justify taking him out. It was one thing to make sure he couldn't have a position of power in town anymore, but kill him? Even we had a code to follow. At the end of the day, we had to be able to live with ourselves. I didn't want to look in the mirror and see a murderer. If I was taking out the trash, then it was just another day. And yes, the sheriff was dirty as fuck, but I wanted to know exactly how bad it was.

"Rabbit, I want you to dig deeper into the sheriff's financials," I instructed, my gaze locked onto his jittery form. "Find out where the money's coming from and where it's going. And don't be afraid to follow any leads, no matter how small or insignificant they might seem."

"Got it, Cheshire," Rabbit muttered, his brow furrowed as he processed the information. I knew he wouldn't let me down. His meticulous nature would ensure every stone was turned and every detail scrutinized. It actually made him ideal for several jobs.

"And, Carpenter," I continued, turning my attention to the towering figure next to Rabbit. "It's time to put some pressure on the sheriff's associates. Make them talk, figure out what they know about his connections and operations. Just don't tip our hand. If they seem like the type who'd be on his side, then make it seem like we want in on the action. Even if the idea of it sickens me."

"Understood," Carpenter grunted, his scowl deepening as he clenched his fists. I could see the hunger for action burning in his eyes.

"Good," I said, nodding my approval. "We've got to be smart about this. The stakes are too damn high." My mind raced with thoughts of just how deep this corruption went, and the danger it posed to not only our club but the entire city. Every one of us was caught in a web of deceit, and it was up to us to unravel it before it strangled us all. "Let's get to work!"

As Rabbit and Carpenter nodded in agreement, I knew that together, we would bring down the corrupt empire that had poisoned our streets and endangered the lives of those closest to us. And when the dust settled, the Underland MC would rise above it all, stronger than ever.

I had one potential ace up my sleeve, and tonight I'd find out if he was on board. I needed eyes on the inside and couldn't think of anyone better.

* * *

The night swallowed the city whole, its darkness wrapping around every street and alley. I stood in the shadows, my back pressed against the cold brick wall of a crumbling warehouse. Pulling out my phone, I punched in Park's number.

"Cheshire?" Park's voice crackled through the line, wary but curious.

"Park, we need to talk," I said, cutting straight to the chase. "I've got some dirt on Sheriff Holmes that'll make your fucking head spin."

"Jesus, Cheshire, what did you get yourself into

this time?" He sighed, his concern for me apparent even through the static.

"Meet me at the old rail yard in an hour." I hung up before he could respond, knowing that deep down, Park was as eager for justice as I was. He just needed a little push. Well, that and I needed to fully remove the blinders he had on when it came to his boss.

With the meeting set, I shot a quick text to Rabbit and Carpenter, letting them know to start the surveillance on Sheriff Holmes' known associates. We had to move fast if we wanted to catch these bastards red-handed.

As I slipped through the darkened streets, I couldn't help but think about all the lives ruined by Sheriff Holmes, and something told me we hadn't even dug through half the crap he'd done. My gut churned with anger, fueling my resolve to bring the corrupt bastard down.

Rabbit and Carpenter were already in position when I arrived at our stakeout spot, their eyes glued to the binoculars as they observed the comings and goings at one of the sheriff's favorite watering holes. I hunkered down beside them, my own gaze narrowing as I watched the seedy characters entering and leaving the bar.

"Anything juicy yet?" I asked, my voice barely above a whisper.

"Caught a couple of his known cronies chatting up some girls earlier," Carpenter replied, his voice tight with disgust. "Might be worth keeping an eye on them. Can't be sure, but they looked a bit on the young side."

"Good." I nodded, my jaw clenched in determination. "We'll follow them. See if they lead us to something we can use against the sheriff. Even if they don't, we'll gather any dirt we can on them as well. I want all of them to pay, and I want them gone."

As we trailed the suspects, I couldn't shake the feeling that our actions were setting off a chain reaction -- one that would ultimately lead to a reckoning for Sheriff Holmes and his corrupt empire. And when it all came crashing down, me and my brothers would be standing tall amidst the rubble, ready to rebuild from the ashes.

When it didn't look like they were going to give us much, I broke off from Rabbit and Carpenter. I glanced at my phone and saw a message from Park. *Can't meet until later.* Which meant I'd have to wait until he texted again.

There was another place I needed to check. If those men were after young girls, and we'd found decent evidence that the sheriff was into trafficking, then I needed to find out more on my own. And there was one place anyone in need could go…

The shelter's walls were cracked and worn, like the souls of those who sought refuge within them. As I stepped inside, the scent of despair hung heavy in the air, making my chest tighten with a mix of rage and sorrow.

"Cheshire?" A voice pulled me from my thoughts, and I turned to see Sister Mary, her eyes filled with a somber kindness that spoke volumes. She ran the shelter, offering solace and protection to those who had been chewed up and spit out by life.

"Need some info, Sister," I said, my tone serious. "Any victims come through here recently? Ones that might've crossed paths with Sheriff Holmes?"

She hesitated, then nodded slowly. "There've been a few. I'll introduce you, but please be gentle with them. They've been through hell."

"Understood." My resolve strengthened as we made our way through the cramped, dimly lit halls to a small room where several women huddled together, their eyes haunted by memories they couldn't escape.

"Girls, this is Cheshire," Sister Mary said. "He wants to ask you some questions about your experiences. He's trying to help put an end to all this."

I crouched down, keeping my voice low and steady. "I promise I won't hurt you or make you relive anything too painful. Just need to know if any of y'all have seen this man before." I held up a photo of Sheriff Holmes, his cold eyes staring back at me.

A few of the women shook their heads, but one girl, barely more than skin and bones, hesitantly raised her hand. "I... I know him," she whispered, her voice trembling.

"Can you tell me anything about what he did? Anything that might help me nail that sick bastard?" I asked, hoping for a breakthrough.

"Y-yes," she stammered, tears welling in her eyes. "He... He was there when they brought me to the warehouse. He watched as... as they did things..." Her voice broke, and I could see the torment etched on her face. My blood boiled with fury.

"Thank you," I told her gently, offering a small, reassuring smile. "You're helping put an end to this horror."

I knew I needed more details from her, but it would have to wait. She seemed too fragile right now. If I poked and prodded, I could end up doing more harm than good. Poor thing. I wished I had a way to make it all better for her, but I wasn't sure even time would be enough to heal her.

A message from Rabbit had me hauling ass a few blocks away. I found them crouched in the shadows outside a decrepit building, waiting for the secret meeting of Sheriff Holmes' associates to begin.

"Ready?" Rabbit asked, his eyes flickering with anticipation.

"Let's do it," I replied, my pulse quickening as we slipped inside, our footsteps silent as we moved through the darkness. We knew we had to be smart, cunning -- one wrong move, and we'd be caught or worse, dead.

As the voices of Sheriff Holmes' associates grew louder, we crept closer, hiding behind stacks of crates and machinery, our ears straining to catch every word. They spoke of their vile deeds, of the suffering they dealt in, and my heart clenched with disgust and determination.

"What happened to that little bitch from the other day?" one of them asked. "She was nice and tight."

"Little whore ran off. Probably with that nun. Besides, she's too broken now. Give her time to heal some. Then we can grab her again." The men laughed and bile rose in my throat. "Once we've got her firmly under control, she'll fetch a nice price."

They talked a bit longer. Once it seemed like they weren't going to incriminate themselves anymore, we backed off.

"Got it all on tape," I whispered to my brothers, the damning evidence clenched tightly in my hand. This was it -- the key to bringing down the monster that had tormented so many innocent souls.

And as we slipped away, unnoticed by those who wallowed in their own filth and depravity, I couldn't help but grin -- my Cheshire grin, fierce and defiant in the face of evil.

As we got on our bikes, I motioned to Rabbit and

Carpenter. "One more stop. Got a name. Gregory Mitchell. He's in the city planning office. From what I've found, he helps arrange the hidey-holes where they stash their victims."

"Let's pay Mr. Mitchell a visit, then," Carpenter chimed in, cracking his knuckles menacingly.

We found him in a seedy dive bar, drunk enough to make him an easy target but still sober enough to make sense. Sliding into the booth across from him, I fixed Gregory with my Cheshire grin, the one that made people squirm and loosen their tongues.

"Evening, Gregory," I drawled, enjoying the way his eyes widened with fear. "Care to tell us about your side gig? The one involving Sheriff Holmes?"

"Wh-what are you talking about?" he stammered, his gaze darting around the room.

"Come on," I coaxed, leaning in closer, my voice dripping with false sympathy. "You're in deep, aren't you? You help him set up his little... operations. But you don't want to be a part of it anymore, do you?"

If what I'd found was true, this man was scared shitless and wanted out. Just one problem... the sheriff wasn't going to let him go. His bottom lip quivered, and I knew I had him.

"I can't," he whispered hoarsely. "He'll kill me."

"Or we could," Rabbit said, his voice low and dangerous.

"Or," I offered, my tone light and conversational, "you could give us the information we need to bring him down, and we'll make sure you're protected. Your choice."

It didn't take long for him to spill everything, revealing the location of one of Sheriff Holmes' secret hideouts. We left him there, trembling and broken, as we headed toward the unmarked warehouse he had described.

"Be ready," I warned my brothers, as we approached the door. "No telling what we'll find inside."

The horrors that lay within were worse than I ever imagined. Cages filled with terrified, malnourished victims, their eyes wide and pleading. The stench of decay and despair hung heavy in the air, making me want to retch.

"Document everything," I commanded, my heart aching for these innocent souls trapped in this hell.

Rabbit and Carpenter moved quickly, snapping photos of the living nightmare before us. Every image captured was another nail in Sheriff Holmes' coffin -- and I'd see to it myself that the bastard would pay.

As we led the survivors out into the night, I couldn't help but feel a grim satisfaction settling in my chest. We were one step closer to bringing down the monster that had plagued our city for far too long. And God help anyone who tried to stand in our way.

But I had to admit, I wanted to see the look on his face when he realized we'd released all his precious victims. Now we just had to figure out what to do with them. Maybe Sister Mary would be able to help. It wasn't like we did this sort of thing all the time. We didn't have protocols in place, and I sure the fuck hoped we never needed to.

* * *

The light of a flickering streetlamp cast eerie shadows on the pavement as I stood by my bike, waiting for Park. The bastard had finally texted saying he was ready to meet. The wind howled through the empty streets. My gut churned with anticipation and a grim determination that gnawed at my insides.

"Cheshire," Park called out, his voice cutting

through the darkness. "You got something for me?"

"More than you're ready for," I replied, handing him a folder filled with damning evidence. His eyes widened as he flipped through the photos, his face pale and sickened.

"Jesus Christ," he whispered, disbelief etched in his features. "This is… this is beyond fucked up."

"Tell me about it," I muttered, feeling the weight of responsibility settling on my shoulders. "But we've got a plan. We expose that bastard Holmes to the public, make sure every Goddamn person knows what he's been up to."

"Count me in," Park said without hesitation. "What do you need me to do?"

"Keep your eyes open, watch our backs. We're making moves, stirring things up. Holmes' goons will be out for blood." My gaze met his, a silent plea for trust and understanding. I knew he was a deputy, and as such siding with us could be badif the sheriff had even an inkling of Park's involvement.

"All right." He nodded, determination hardening his expression. "Let's bring this fucker down."

I briefed Park on our strategy, every calculated move designed to corner Sheriff Holmes and dismantle his criminal empire. Even though I trusted him for the most part, I wasn't sure I wanted to fill him in on everything yet. Being told the mayor's office was part of this shitstorm might be more than he could handle right now. With each step, I felt the noose tightening around the monster who'd terrorized our city for far too long.

Carpenter and Rabbit joined us. I could tell they weren't sure how to feel about Park being included. I couldn't blame them. Here we were trying to take down the sheriff and now we had one of his deputies lending us a hand. I could admit it seemed like a horrible idea, but in my gut, I knew we could trust Park.

"Ready?" I asked my brothers, their faces set with resolve.

"Born ready." Rabbit smirked, cracking his knuckles.

"Let's do this," Carpenter chimed in, revving his engine.

We rode through the night, our bikes roaring like thunder, hearts pounding with adrenaline. We knew what was at stake, and failure wasn't an option. As we neared a hideout where crucial evidence was rumored to be stashed, the hairs on the back of my neck stood up -- something felt off.

"Watch out!" I shouted, just as bullets ripped through the air, narrowly missing us as we skidded to a stop and dove for cover.

"Shit!" Rabbit cursed, his eyes wild with fury. "Holmes' boys were waiting for us!"

"Stay low and move fast," I ordered, my mind racing with strategy and tactics. "We need that evidence!"

As the firefight intensified, we darted between crates and dumpsters, our lives hanging by a thread. I could feel the heat of the bullets whizzing past my face, but fear had no place in this fight.

"Got it!" Carpenter yelled, clutching a black duffel bag tightly to his chest. I wasn't going to question how he'd managed to grab it so fast. Not right now at any rate. "Let's get the fuck out of here!"

"Go, go, go!" I barked, leading the charge as we sprinted toward our bikes. The sound of sirens filled the air, drowning out the gunfire and chaos around us.

Thanks, Park. I had no doubt he'd called in the

deputies. Hopefully the good ones, like him.

"See you in hell, you bastards!" I shouted over the roar of our engines, knowing we'd struck a fatal blow against Sheriff Holmes and his criminal operation.

With every mile we put between us and that nightmare, I felt a fierce satisfaction burning inside me. No matter the cost, I swore we'd bring justice to those who'd suffered under Holmes' reign of terror.

And I'd die before I let anyone stand in our way.

Chapter Five

Eliza

The room spun as I cowered in the corner, my arms protectively covering my head. Glass shards flew through the air. My father's rage was a tornado, leaving destruction and chaos in its wake. I should stop replacing the breakable items in my room, but since I spent so much time here, I liked having pretty things around me. It made my prison a little more bearable.

"Please, stop!" I whimpered, tears streaming down my face. But there was no mercy to be found in his cold eyes. He loomed over me, his fists clenched like steel hammers. I didn't know what happened, but he'd come home furious.

"Shut up!" he snarled, striking me hard across the face. Pain exploded through my skull, and I tasted blood in my mouth. My head slammed against the wall, stars dancing in my vision.

I could feel my body trembling, the urge to scream clawing at my throat. But I held it in. Screaming only made him angrier.

"Look at you," he sneered, grabbing my hair and yanking my head back. "Pathetic. You're just like your mother -- weak and useless."

"Please, I'm sorry," I gasped, choking on my own fear. But he didn't care. His fist connected with my stomach, driving the breath from my lungs. The pain radiated through me like wildfire, but I forced myself to stay conscious. If I passed out, he might think I was dead. With my luck, he'd bury me alive.

"Next time," he growled, his voice low and dangerous, "you won't be so lucky." The threat hung heavy in the air, a noose tightening around my neck. I knew, deep down, that one day he would make good on that promise.

As he finally stepped away, I curled up into a tight ball, trembling sobs racking my battered body. I could still feel the weight of his cold gaze, like a predator stalking its prey. And I knew time was running out. Something had to change. I couldn't keep living like this -- a life that was nothing but pain, fear, and darkness.

"Remember what I said," he whispered. And as he left the room, slamming the door behind him, I knew my only chance at survival was to escape. Somehow, some way, I had to get away from him -- no matter the cost.

I heard his steps as he went downstairs, and I listened intently. It didn't take long before the front door opened and shut. Although, he'd tricked me before. This time, I waited. Staring at the clock, I watched as the minutes ticked by. When another fifteen passed, I thought he'd really left.

My heart thundered in my chest, like a wild animal caged and desperate for escape. I knew this was my chance, the only one I might get. With shaky hands, I wiped away the tears that stained my cheeks. Time to run.

I forced myself up, every bruise screaming in protest. I had to move now, while he was gone. I crept to the door, my breath shallow and ragged. The wood felt cold against my palm as I leaned into it, listening once more for any sound of movement in the house. When it remained silent, I turned the handle, wincing at the soft *creak* it made.

The hallway stretched before me, shadows looming like silent specters. I hugged the walls, feet barely making a sound as I padded across the floor.

Fear clawed at my insides, threatening to choke me, but I couldn't stop. Not now.

Every tiny noise set my nerves on edge, my instincts sharpening with each passing second. The hum of the refrigerator, the distant howl of a dog -- all seemed deafening in my heightened state of awareness. But I couldn't afford to falter, not even for a moment.

My resolve hardened, fueled by the burning desire for freedom. I couldn't let him win, not this time. My breath hitched as I reached the back door, the cold metal handle slick with sweat from my trembling hands. One more step, and I'd be outside, away from this nightmare. But I knew it wouldn't be easy, that there were still obstacles waiting in the darkness.

"Please, please, please," I repeated like a mantra, praying that luck would be on my side for once. And as I slipped through the door and into the night, I felt a flicker of hope, a tiny spark in the depths of my soul.

"Almost there," I whispered to myself, the chill air stinging my battered skin. "Just a little farther."

But even as I spoke, I knew that the real struggle was just beginning -- and that the road ahead was paved with danger, uncertainty, and the ghosts of my past.

The night swallowed me whole. Step by step, I inched farther from the house of horrors I had once called home. My heart thudded against my ribcage. Every snap of a twig or rustle of leaves threatening to shatter my fragile composure.

"Can't screw this up," I muttered under my breath, desperation driving me forward like a puppet on strings. "Just have to keep moving."

And then it happened -- the distant roar of motorcycles shattered the quiet night, the sound echoing through the air like thunder. My body froze, blood in my veins turning to ice. Friend or foe? Underland MC or something else?

"Shit," I whispered, hugging the shadows of a large oak tree as the rumbling grew louder. Panic clawed at the edges of my mind, threatening to tear me apart. If it was the Underland MC, maybe they'd help me. Maria had seemed confident they would. But what if they were just another bunch of sadistic assholes? I couldn't trust anyone these days but going it alone... that was a death sentence.

Every second wasted felt like an eternity, each heartbeat a ticking time bomb waiting to explode. *Help might not come again.* I waited and watched, fear pinning me in place. *But they could betray me...* The thought made me want to vomit, bile rising in my throat as I considered the consequences of trusting the wrong people.

"Fuck it," I whispered, clenching my fists and bracing for impact. "Either way, I'm screwed."

The motorcycles drew closer, the ground beneath me vibrating with the raw power of their engines. It was now or never -- trust the unknown or face the monsters I knew all too well. Even if the engines I heard weren't from the Underland MC, *anything* had to be better than this miserable existence. My breath hitched, and I made my choice. My legs trembled as I clung to the oak tree, poised to make a split-second decision that could either save or doom me.

"Fuck, fuck, fuck," I whispered under my breath, cold sweat trickling down my spine as I hesitated, torn between the devil I knew and the unknown danger that lurked before me.

"Damn, girl, you look like you've seen a ghost," said a voice, smooth and confident, laced with a hint of amusement. My eyes flicked to the speaker -- Cheshire. His mischievous grin was plastered on his face, his piercing blue eyes sizing me up. The aura of cunning radiating from him made me shudder. But once he got a better look at my face, the smile dropped from his face.

"Shit," he muttered. "What the hell?"

My gaze swept over the other members of the Underland MC, each one a study in raw intimidation. Hatter towered above the rest, his scarred face and piercing eyes speaking of a life forged in violence. His calm, calculated demeanor sent a chill down my spine, and I couldn't shake the feeling he was capable of both great mercy and unspeakable brutality.

"Think the sheriff got to her too?" one of them whispered.

They knew about my dad? From the way he'd spoken just now, I had to assume that meant they'd help me.

"Easy there," Cheshire said, holding up his hands in mock surrender. "We're not here to hurt you."

"Then what do you want?" I asked, desperately trying to maintain control of the situation. My mind raced with a thousand different scenarios, each darker than the last. I'd thought they may help me, but I had to wonder… why were they here?

"Look, we heard about your father," Hatter said, his voice measured and steady. His gaze scanned my face and exposed arms. I knew what he saw. The bruises, scars, and fresh cuts. "We don't want you to suffer at his hands any longer."

"How do I know for sure I can trust you? And how did you know he's my father?" My gaze flicked from one biker to another. The way they looked at me -

- like predators sizing up their prey -- made my skin crawl.

Cheshire inched a little closer. "We've done our research on the sheriff. He's into some bad shit. Honestly, it doesn't surprise me he'd beat the hell out of his daughter. You're Eliza, right?"

I nodded. It looked like they really had been looking into my father. But that still didn't explain how they knew about me. Although, it was true he didn't exactly keep me a secret. He still kept me as hidden as possible. People would ask too many questions if I went out in public, thanks to all the bruises and cuts on my body. Some had left permanent scars.

"What do you know about me?" I asked.

Cheshire moved a little closer, his hands up as if trying to reassure me he wouldn't harm me. "We have someone in the club who knows how to access certain files and records. Found your birth certificate but not anything showing you'd died. I'm curious why the town doesn't talk about you, though."

I licked my lips. "My dad told everyone I'm sick, that I need to stay home. He homeschooled me, or rather once I got old enough to figure most of it out on my own, he enrolled me in a program and then gave me the materials so I could teach myself."

"So you've never gone to school or made friends?" Cheshire asked.

I paused. There was one person I'd seen a few times in passing. One of my father's deputies. He'd seemed nice. The three times I'd met him had been here at the house, during a period when my father wasn't leaving bruises in obvious places. It had been a while since I'd seen him. "No, I haven't."

I couldn't really consider someone I met a handful of times to be a friend, right? It wasn't like we spoke on the phone or exchanged letters. My father never would have allowed such a thing. I scanned the street, knowing it wouldn't be long before he returned. Standing out here was dangerous. My gaze landed on Maria's house. After she'd been treated at the hospital, she hadn't returned. I hoped she was all right.

"Your choice," Hatter said, his gaze locked on mine.

"Choice? For what?" I asked, having lost track of the conversation. I'd been too focused on Cheshire.

"Stay here and face him, or take a chance with us," Hatter said. "But I promise you this -- we won't betray you."

"Promises don't mean much. They're easily broken," I mumbled, my mind racing with doubt and desperation. Every fiber of my being screamed for me to run, yet something in Hatter's eyes held me in place. A glimmer of hope? Or just another cruel trick?

"Time's running out, girl," Cheshire warned, his tone darkening. He scanned the area much like I had. Was he worried my father would be back? "What's it going to be?"

Taking a deep breath and stepping out of the shadows, my heart pounded. I had made my choice -- now all that remained was to face the consequences.

"Eliza, you don't have to be scared. We're not here to hurt you." Hatter gave me a slight smile.

"Easy for you to say," I muttered, hugging myself, trying to make myself smaller. "You aren't the one who's been beaten black and blue."

"True," he conceded, his eyes flicking over my bruised face. "But we've seen our fair share of pain too."

"It doesn't mean I can trust you any more than I can trust him."

His gaze never wavered, but I could see the conflict in his eyes, like he understood my hesitation but couldn't afford to let it sway him. And if he was torn, what hope did that leave for me?

"Think about it," he urged, nodding toward the other bikers. "We've got your back, Eliza. You just got to take that first step."

"Take a step?" I scoffed, bile rising in my throat. "And then what? You turn on me? Or maybe you're secretly working for my father."

"Wouldn't blame you for thinking that," he admitted. "But we aren't like your father. We live by a code."

"Right. A code. Of course, you do. And how do I know that code won't get me killed?"

"Can't promise that," he said, his expression grave. "But I can promise we'll do everything in our power to keep you safe."

"Everything?" I whispered, my voice barely audible over the pounding of my heart.

"Everything," he repeated, his eyes locked on mine.

I hesitated, torn between the burning need for safety and the cold grip of fear that refused to let me go. But as I looked into Hatter's eyes, I saw something that made me believe -- if only for a moment -- that maybe, just maybe, they could be my salvation.

"All right," I murmured, taking a shaky step toward the motorcycles. "I'll go with you."

"Good choice," Hatter said, nodding in approval.

"Can you walk?" Cheshire asked. "I realize you've made it this far, but... no offense, you don't seem too steady right now."

Why was he being so nice to me? I gave him a nod. "I can make it."

He held out his hand, and I hesitantly took it. Cheshire led me over to the bikes, and my heart pounded with a mix of fear and hope, each beat a reminder of the risk I was taking. But in that moment, it was a risk I was willing to take.

"All right, then," Hatter said, breaking the silence. He gestured toward an empty bike next to him. "Hop on."

"Are… are you sure?" I asked, glancing nervously at the imposing machine.

"Positive," he replied, his voice steady and reassuring.

Cheshire came closer, and without sparing me a glance, threw his leg over the machine and settled on the seat. With a shaky breath, I lifted my leg over the bike, settling down onto the worn leather seat behind him. I gripped the sides of his leather vest, worried I might fall. He tensed but didn't say or do anything. I had to admit, I was glad he was the one I'd be riding with.

He started the bike and the motorcycle's powerful engine rumbled between my thighs, sending tremors through my body.

"Ready?" Hatter asked, his hand on the throttle. I looked into his eyes, finding a strange sense of comfort in their depths.

"Y-yeah," I stammered, gripping Cheshire tightly. "Let's go."

"Good," Hatter said with a nod. "Whatever you do, don't let go."

"I've got her, Pres," Cheshire said. I felt the light touch of his hand against mine. For some reason, I found that small gesture reassuring. What was it about him that made me feel like everything would be fine?

Hatter pulled off first, and Cheshire fell in

behind him, pulling up next to him after we were a block away. The world seemed to blur together as we sped down the road, the wind whipping through my hair and tearing at my clothes. For a moment, I felt free -- free from the pain, free from the fear.

But as the road stretched on before us, I couldn't help but wonder what lay ahead. I had placed my trust in these men, in the Underland MC, but would it be enough? Or was I simply trading one hell for another?

"Eliza," Hatter shouted over the roar of the engines, snapping me back to reality. "Don't look back."

"Why? Is he behind us?" I asked, my heart pounding.

Cheshire patted my leg. "Everything's fine, Eliza. He means to look ahead and forget your past. Your dad can't hurt you now."

And so, I didn't. I looked forward, into the darkness, and let the night swallow me whole.

* * *

By the time we reached the clubhouse, my adrenaline had worn off. Fatigue pulled at me, and every part of my body ached. Riding on a motorcycle probably hadn't been the best idea considering how battered and bruised I was. Cheshire helped me off the bike and my knees balked. He put his arms around my waist and led me into the clubhouse. A few people were inside and they stopped to stare. They probably wondered why he'd brought home a stray.

"Take a seat for a minute," Cheshire said, guiding me over to a couch.

I sank onto the cushions and nearly groaned from how much I hurt. Someone brought over a bottle of water and handed it to me. I accepted and stared at it for a moment.

"It's safe," Cheshire said. He took it from me and cracked the seal, then tipped his head back and poured a little into his mouth without letting it touch his lips. "See, no drugs in it."

My cheeks warmed. "I wasn't thinking that."

He smirked. "Liar. But it's understandable."

Hatter came over and clapped Cheshire on the back. "Watch over her. I'll get someone to make sure the empty bedroom has clean sheets and towels. I'm sure she'd like to lie down and rest."

He was right. That sounded like heaven. "Thank you. Are you sure it's not too much trouble? I honestly didn't think much further than getting away from my dad. Where I'd stay, how I'd pay for things... I never really sorted it all out."

Cheshire hunkered down in front of me, taking my hand. "You don't have to worry about all that. You're welcome to stay here as long as you want. And there's no charge for anything you need or use."

It seemed almost too good to be true, but I gave him a nod before swallowing some of the water. Hatter walked off, leaving me alone with Cheshire, and the stares of two people over by the bar. I wasn't sure who everyone was, but it didn't matter right now. Even if they told me, I wouldn't remember. My brain felt all fuzzy. Too much had happened today.

Hatter returned a short while later. "All set. I'll let Cheshire show you where to go."

"Thank you. For everything," I said.

"It's no trouble, Eliza. Just rest and heal."

Cheshire helped me stand, and I followed him down a hall to a closed door. He pushed it open and I saw a small bedroom. I wasn't sure how much longer I could remain standing. My body swayed, and I knew the moment I lay down and closed my eyes, I'd fall asleep.

"If you need anything, just open the door and call out," Cheshire said. "You're safe, Eliza. No one is going to hurt you. Get some sleep, and hopefully you'll feel better in the morning."

Chapter Six

Eliza

The room swam into focus as I opened my eyes, a dull ache pounding at the back of my skull. I blinked, trying to clear the haze from my vision. Where the hell was I?

"Easy," a voice murmured nearby. Cheshire. The one who'd pulled me out of that hellhole.

My heart jackhammered in my chest as I realized I was lying on a bed in a strange room. What happened to me? I remembered the Underland MC taking me with them. Vaguely recalled going to their clubhouse, and then... I'd been shown to a room. But what else had happened? Why was everything so fuzzy?

"Where..." My voice cracked, barely a whisper.

"Underland MC clubhouse," Cheshire answered, his grin not quite reaching his eyes. "You're safe here. Do you remember anything from last night? You walked to this room on your own two feet."

"A little," I said. "I remember you bringing me to the clubhouse on your motorcycle, but everything after that is foggy. It's like the memories are there but not, if that makes any sense."

"Don't look so terrified," Cheshire said. "And yes, it makes sense. You were under a lot of stress. Maybe more than your mind could handle or process."

I winced. Wasn't that the type of thing someone said in a horror movie right before you died? "I think you need to work on your bedside manner. Or at least the delivery. That phrase is..."

He snorted. "I'm not some psycho killer. Well, I guess technically I'm a killer. I was active duty in a war zone after all. My hands aren't clean, but I'd never hurt an innocent person."

I struggled to sit up in the bed and he held out his hand for me. I grabbed hold and swung my legs over the side, managing to stand.

"Um, where's…"

"Bathroom?" he asked. I nodded. "The closed door over there."

I looked in the direction he'd pointed and saw a door in the darkened corner of the room. Hurrying over, I locked myself inside to relieve my aching bladder and splash some water on my face. I winced with every move I made, the bruises and cuts reminding me of what I'd been through.

When I came out, I felt slightly more settled. I'd escaped my father, even if I didn't know how long I'd be able to stay hidden from him. Sooner or later, someone would tell him they saw me with the Underland MC. There was no way we'd made it from my house to here without anyone noticing.

Cheshire gave me a warm smile, one completely different from the sarcastic one he seemed to wear most of the time. I moved closer to him, until I could feel the heat of his body. Whatever scent he wore teased my nose, and I nearly closed my eyes and breathed him in.

With Cheshire's hand on my back, I found myself being guided from the room and into the main part of the clubhouse. The buzz of conversation died down as the bikers watched me with curiosity. We reached a table where Hatter sat, his presence demanding attention even when he wasn't speaking. My hands shook a little as I sank into a seat next to Cheshire, feeling the weight of everyone's gazes on me.

"Eliza," Hatter said, his eyes locked onto mine, almost as if he were digging into my soul and searching for something. I wondered what he'd find.

Most likely a scared girl, still trying to make sense of it all.

"Welcome," he continued, leaning back in his chair, a hint of a smile in his voice. "The room you woke up in is yours for however long you need or want it. I'm sure Cheshire will give you the tour later."

"And my father?"

"We'll do everything we can to protect you."

"Thanks," I muttered. I noticed he hadn't guaranteed I'd make it out of this alive. He was smart. Doing his best was one thing. Promising I'd be fine was another. My father had probably discovered I was missing. It wouldn't be long before he started hunting me like an animal.

"Try to relax, sweetheart," Cheshire murmured, his thumb rubbing gently against my hand. It was a small gesture, but it meant a hell of a lot, coming from him. "You're one of us now."

I glanced around the room, seeing everyone in a new light. Could I really call these people my... what? Friends? Would they even want me to? We were strangers. It made me wonder why Cheshire would make such a statement after only meeting me last night.

"Welcome to Underland, Eliza," Hatter said again, his voice steady and calming. "We'll make sure you don't regret it."

"Thanks," I whispered, finally meeting his gaze again. There was something hypnotizing about those eyes, like they were casting a spell over me. And for the first time since waking up in this strange new world, I felt a glimmer of hope.

Maybe, just maybe, I could survive this.

I swallowed hard, trying to steady my nerves as Cheshire began introducing me to the others. "This here's Eliza," he said, his voice casual but confident. "She's going to be staying with us for a while."

"Eliza, meet Knave." Cheshire gestured to a burly man, ink covering every inch of his arms. Knave nodded at me. The man looked a bit scary, but I knew better than to judge a book by its cover.

Carpenter was next, then Rabbit, who was a wiry man with a nervous smile. He gave me a quick nod, his gaze lingering on me just a bit too long for comfort. It made me feel like he saw far more than I wanted him to.

"And finally, we have Tweedle," Cheshire said, motioning to a man leaning against the wall with a beer in his hand. "You'll have to meet the others later."

"Nice to meet y'all," I mumbled.

"Likewise," Knave drawled.

Just then, a woman approached the table, her fragile frame belying the strength in her eyes. She offered me reassuring smile that made my heart slow just a touch. "Hey, Eliza," she said gently. "My name's Jo. Welcome to Underland."

"Thanks," I replied, finding some comfort in her presence. She looked like she knew what it was like to be afraid, to feel hunted. Although, the fact she was perfectly at ease around these men spoke volumes. If she felt safe here, then I could too.

"Can I get you something to eat?" Jo asked, her voice quiet but strong. I could tell she was trying to make me feel welcome, and it meant a lot.

"Sure," I said, smiling weakly back at her. "That'd be nice."

As Jo went to get me some food, I watched the others, their reactions to me still a mix of curiosity and concern.

Jo returned to the table, a steaming bowl of

something that smelled like heaven in her hands. She set it down in front of me, along with a bottle of water.

"Are you okay, Eliza?" she asked, sitting down next to me. "You need anything for the pain?"

"Uh, no, I'm all right," I replied, trying to sound braver than I felt. I glanced at Cheshire, who looked like he was listening to every word even though his gaze was on Hatter. Over the counter meds didn't do much for me anymore. They'd barely take the edge off for thirty minutes.

"Good," Jo said, still speaking quietly. "Just let me know if there's anything you need, okay? We're here to help you."

"Thanks," I whispered, taking a bite of the warm, slightly salty food and letting it soothe me from the inside out. It wasn't much, but it was something, and right now that meant everything.

As I ate, I couldn't help but notice the silent communication between Cheshire and Hatter. Their eyes met for a brief moment, and then Cheshire leaned in close, his breath tickling my ear.

"Listen, Eliza," he said, his voice low and steady. "I know you're scared, and you've got every right to be. But we're going to make sure your dad can't get his hands on you again. You aren't alone anymore."

Something deep within me unclenched, just a little bit. I barely knew these people, but they seemed to genuinely care, and that was enough for now. I nodded, not trusting myself to speak without crying.

"Thank you," I managed eventually, my voice trembling only slightly. Cheshire just squeezed my shoulder and looked away. It only took me a moment to realize he was doing it for my benefit. With so many eyes locked on me, I felt like a bug under a microscope.

As I finished my meal, I tried to focus on the

conversation around me, on the laughter and the camaraderie of these strangers who were offering me protection. It was an odd mix of comfort and fear, but it was better than being alone, better than feeling like a hunted animal with nowhere to turn.

I felt like I could learn to trust them -- especially Cheshire, with his piercing blue eyes and that damn grin that made my heart race every time I looked at him.

Watching these rough men laugh and bust each other's balls, I could feel something shift inside me. It was like a tiny spark of hope flickering to life, and even though I knew it might be snuffed out any second, I clung to it. It was the first time I'd felt relieved in so very long.

"Eliza," Jo whispered, leaning closer so we wouldn't be overheard. "I know this all seems crazy, but you can trust these guys. They saved my life when I thought there was no way out."

"Really?" I asked, my voice shaking just a bit less now.

"Swear on my life." She nodded, her eyes sincere. "Hatter and the others, they're good men. They want Warren to be safe. They'll help you, just like they helped me."

"Thank you," I whispered back, feeling that little spark grow stronger. If they'd done it for Jo, maybe they could do it for me too. It seemed like Maria had been right about the Underland MC.

"Hey, Jo, tell Eliza about that time Hatter kicked Tweedle's ass in pool," Cheshire chimed in, his grin wide as ever.

"Ah, that was classic." Jo laughed, and the story spilled out, painting a picture of a night filled with laughter, competition, and camaraderie.

As they talked, I couldn't help but feel a sense of protectiveness surrounding me. These people, these bikers who looked like they could snap me in half without breaking a sweat, were offering me shelter and safety -- and not just because they felt sorry for me or something.

No, they wanted to make things right. To fix what was broken in this town, one piece at a time. And I knew my father was a huge piece they'd need to deal with. If they could take him off the board, then it would be a game changer for them.

"Eliza, remember this," Jo said, her hand covering mine. "You're not alone anymore."

As the room buzzed with conversation and laughter, I knew she was right. I had these people at my back, and together, we were going to face whatever came our way.

And for the first time in a long while, that tiny spark of hope inside me burned bright and strong.

At some point, Cheshire had gotten up. I watched as he moved around the room, chatting and joking with the others. There was a magnetic pull to him, like he was the center of gravity in this place. My cheeks burned something fierce, and I prayed no one noticed.

"Hey, Eliza," said Jo, snapping me out of my thoughts. "You good?"

"Y-yeah, I'm fine," I stammered, feeling like an idiot for staring at Cheshire like that.

"Good. You'll fit in here just fine," she reassured me with a gentle smile.

"Thanks, Jo." I gave her a weak smile, hoping I looked more confident than I felt.

"Come on, let's grab a drink," she suggested, leading me over to the bar. The cold bottle felt good in my hand, helping to steady my nerves.

"Here's to new beginnings," Jo toasted, clinking her Coke against mine.

"New beginnings," I echoed, taking a swig. It was bitter but refreshing, and it helped banish some of the heat from my cheeks.

"Eliza, come over here," Cheshire called out, waving me over to where he stood with Hatter and a couple of the others. My heart did a little dance in my chest, and I swallowed hard, trying to keep my cool.

"All right," I said, steeling myself as I walked over to them. Up close, Cheshire was even more magnetic, his blue eyes sparkling with mischief. I could feel his gaze linger on me, and it made my insides quiver.

Cheshire put his arm around my shoulders when I stopped beside him. I tensed for a brief moment before leaning into him. Maybe my few sips of alcohol had already given me courage. Otherwise, I'd have never been bold enough to do something like this.

"Welcome to the club, Eliza," Rabbit said warmly. "We're glad to have you here."

"Thanks," I replied, trying to sound more at ease than I felt. But with Cheshire standing so close, it was damn near impossible. And why did everyone keep welcoming me to the club? They made it seem like I'd be here forever instead of just temporarily. These people didn't even know me, but they were willing to risk everything for me. Maybe staying longer wouldn't be a bad thing.

As I watched Cheshire laugh and joke with his brothers, I couldn't help but feel a strange sort of yearning. This man, who had barely known me a day, had shown me kindness and protection when I needed it most.

My cheeks flushed again as I realized I was falling for him -- hard. And I was terrified that everyone could see it plain as day. Love at first sight didn't really exist. Did it?

I had a feeling I was in more trouble than I realized.

Chapter Seven

Cheshire

Hatter had told me to stand down, but I couldn't. I'd ridden into town to pick up a few things for Eliza when I'd seen them outside town hall -- Mayor Davis and Robert Lewis. They weren't quite as rotten as the sheriff, but... the two of them made me sick. I was ready to take them all down and bury them six feet under. They were making this town rot.

I'd immediately pulled over, unable to stop myself. Hatter was going to have my ass for this, but I didn't care. My boots echoed off the concrete as I strode down the sidewalk. Mayor Davis and Robert Lewis stood there, smirks plastered on their faces like they owned the place. I wanted to knock those smug expressions off their damn faces. Too many fucking witnesses, though.

"Ah, Cheshire," Mayor Davis drawled, flicking an imaginary speck of dust off his immaculate suit. "What brings you to our humble abode?"

"Cut the shit, Davis," I spat, stepping closer until we were almost nose-to-nose. "We know about your little arrangement with Sheriff Holmes."

"Is that so?" he replied, feigning surprise. "Well, I must say, I'm impressed you managed to uncover that particular tidbit."

"Enough games," I snapped, my temper flaring. "You're going down, and we're going to be the ones to take you there."

"Ha!" Robert Lewis barked, his laughter cold and empty. "You and what army, Cheshire?"

"An old man and a snake don't scare me," I retorted, crossing my arms over my chest. "Especially when they're both crawling in the dirt. You think you're untouchable, but you're wrong."

"Such big words for someone who's clearly out of his depth," Mayor Davis said, his voice dripping with condescension. "But let's not be hasty, Cheshire. I'm willing to make you a deal."

I raised an eyebrow, waiting for him to continue. I only wished I had a way to record this conversation. No way I'd be able to take out my phone and open the recording app.

"Abandon this foolish crusade against Sheriff Holmes, and I'll ensure the Underland MC remains untouched by the law," he offered, his eyes twinkling with mischief.

"Really? That's your grand plan?" I scoffed. "Sell our souls to the devil himself? I'd rather dance with the Reaper than side with scum like you."

"Such loyalty," Robert Lewis sneered. "But what has the Underland MC ever done for you, Cheshire? The club's nothing but a bunch of losers."

"Watch your mouth," I growled, fists clenched at my sides. "The Underland MC is my family. We may be flawed, but we've got each other's backs. Each and every man in the club has served in the military. Those men are heroes. That's more than I can say for you two."

"Your loyalty's misplaced, Cheshire," Mayor Davis insisted, his voice growing more insistent. "Align with us, and you'll have power beyond your wildest dreams."

"Sorry, Davis, but there's not enough money in the world to make me forget who I am," I replied, my voice cold as steel. "I'm an honorable man through and through. No amount of sweet talk can change that. I'd sooner die than become like you."

"Suit yourself," he said, shrugging his shoulders.

"But don't say I didn't offer you a chance. You're making a grave mistake, Cheshire."

"Only grave I see is the one y'all are digging for yourselves," I shot back, turning on my heel and walking away. If I stayed there, I'd take a swing at them, at the very least. Worst case, I'd kill the bastards right here in front of anyone passing by.

I'd often wondered why evil people were put on this earth. I still didn't understand why. All I knew was I'd do whatever I could to get rid of trash like those two. I hadn't survived hell on earth to deal with this shit in my own backyard. Hatter and I had a plan. But before we could implement it, we needed to clean house. Once the sheriff was gone, these two would be next.

Keep walking. Don't look back. Don't do anything stupid.

The air was thick with tension, like the calm before a storm. I could feel it in my bones -- this was far from over. Their gazes were locked on me. I didn't have to see them to know. I could feel it.

"Cheshire," Robert Lewis called out, his voice dripping with venom. "I think it's time we settle this like men."

I paused and glanced over my shoulder. He cracked his knuckles menacingly and stepped forward, a smug grin plastered across his face. Shit. I knew I needed to keep going, to ignore him... but I couldn't.

"Fine by me," I replied, rolling my neck to loosen up. My hands were already itching for a good fight. "But just to be clear, you asked for this. I tried to walk away, and you wouldn't let me."

Robert lunged at me like a caged animal, his fists flying. But I was ready for him. I sidestepped his first punch and delivered a hard jab to his ribs. He grunted in pain, but his eyes never left mine -- filled with rage and determination.

"Is that all you got?" I taunted, ducking under another wild swing. Robert's face was growing red with frustration, and I loved every second of it. He was strong, no doubt about it, but he was slow and predictable. And I'd fought far worse than him in my day.

He came at me again, and I dodged and countered with ease, each of my hits landing with precision. It wasn't long before he was gasping for breath, sweat pouring down his face. I could see the defeat in his eyes, but he refused to back down.

"Enough!" I snapped, grabbing his wrist and twisting it until he cried out in pain. "You're clearly not going to win. Just back down while you still can. Or do I need to put you down?"

I shoved him away, watching as he stumbled and fell to the ground in a heap. As I turned my back on him, I wondered if he took it as the sign of disrespect I intended. You never turned your back on an enemy -- except in this case, I wasn't worried he'd take me down. The fucker was far too weak for that.

I knew I'd have to tell Hatter what happened, and he'd likely chew my ass out. I'd crossed a line. However, the little shit hadn't given me much of a choice. I knew I needed to cover my ass, and fast. I pulled out my phone and shot off a text to March.

Pull camera footage near town hall. I need proof I didn't start the fight with Robert Lewis.

My phone rang almost immediately.

"What the fuck?" March asked the second the call connected.

"Watch what happened. You'll understand. I did my best to walk away. The asshole just wouldn't let me."

"Fine. But you know I have to tell Hatter since you're asking me to do this," he said.

"Yeah. I was going to talk to him when I got back anyway. I grabbed a few things for Eliza. Have one more stop to make before I head back."

"I'll hold off as long as I can, but if he walks by and asks what I'm doing…"

"No worries, March."

I ended the call and got on my bike. I'd picked up some essentials for Eliza, but there was only so much I could fit in my saddlebags. Jo had tried to lend her some clothes, but they weren't close enough to the same size for that to work. I'd told her to order some stuff, and it was being delivered later today, but I wanted to give her some things to make her feel at home right now.

Stopping at a corner market, I ran in and found the magazine section. I had no idea what Eliza liked, so I grabbed a few different types of magazines, then picked up a romance novel. I knew Jo liked them, so I hoped Eliza would too. If nothing else, maybe it would give the two women something to bond over.

Once I'd checked out, I headed back to the clubhouse. I wasn't sure why I felt so drawn to Eliza. Although, anyone could see she was beautiful under the bruises and cuts. It was more than that. Beauty could fade over time. What Eliza had was something else… a magnetic pull I didn't understand, but I wasn't going to question it.

The moment I cleared the doorway, I saw her at a table with Jo. The other woman gave me a wink and hurried off, leaving me alone with Eliza. I set the bags down in front of her.

"I wasn't sure what you liked, but…" I rubbed

the back of my neck. "I, um, just wanted you to feel more like this was your home and less like a temporary resting place."

She gave me a soft smile. "Thanks, Cheshire. No one's ever done something like this for me before. It was sweet of you to think of me."

Not really. I'd done it because I wanted to get closer to her. Hatter was the only one of us with a woman, and after watching him with Jo, I'd started to think that's what was missing in my life. Eliza had dropped into my lap, and it had almost seemed like fate.

"Why don't you put your things away, then meet me back here for a drink? I'd like to learn more about you."

Her cheeks flushed and she gave me a quick nod before hurrying off. She seemed innocent and sweet, the exact opposite of the women I'd dated in the past. Maybe it's why I found her to be so damn cute.

Before Eliza had a chance to return, the doors to the clubhouse slammed open. Mayor Davis, his face a mask of fury, stood with a group of men at his side. They looked like muscle for hire.

"Since you won't listen to reason, Cheshire," he snarled, "I'll have to deal with you and your misguided club another way."

What the absolute fuck? The man had clearly lost his mind. When I'd left him and Lewis on the sidewalk, it never crossed my mind one of them might show up here. Honestly, I hadn't thought they had the balls for it. Seemed like the mayor did.

With a wave of his hand, Mayor Davis signaled for his men to attack, and chaos erupted around us. My brothers and I sprang into action, fists flying and bodies colliding as we fought to defend ourselves and our home.

"Stay focused," I shouted over the din, my knuckles connecting with an attacker's jaw. "We've got each other's backs!"

Despite the intensity of the battle, I couldn't help but feel a surge of pride at how well we were working together. We were united in our cause -- and no amount of threats or violence would ever change that. Besides, after being in combat, this was nothing. If the mayor thought this would scare us off, he was delusional.

Adrenaline surged through my veins, making me feel unstoppable.

"Cheshire, behind you!" Absolem's warning reached my ears just in time, and I ducked, feeling the wind from a punch that would've connected with my face. I countered with a swift uppercut, watching in satisfaction as the bastard dropped.

"Thanks," I grunted, not breaking my focus from the battle. I could hear Eliza's terrified screams in the background, but there was no time to comfort her now. We had to win this fight first. I could only hope she was out of the way.

"Keep it together, boys!" Hatter yelled as I drove my knee into an assailant's gut. The man doubled over in pain, and I finished him off with a powerful right hook. I glanced toward the Pres and saw he was more than handling the men attacking him. Two were already on the floor at his feet.

Why the hell were there so many? It seemed like for every three we took out, more came inside the clubhouse. I'd thought he only had the guys standing with him, but it seemed reinforcements had been outside. The next man I dropped look familiar, and I realized he was a deputy.

"Eliza, stay down!" Knave barked. I turned to find her, and saw Knave kick a man in the head before he could reach Eliza. She pressed tight to the wall, her eyes wide.

"Cheshire, incoming!" Absolem shouted again, and I turned just in time to see a burly man charging toward me, fists clenched. I sidestepped his attack, grabbing his arm and using his momentum to slam him into a nearby wall. His head hit the floor with a sickening *thud*.

"Is that all you got?" I taunted, my breathing ragged but my grin firmly in place. Smiling while beating someone senseless often left them feeling disoriented. But inside, I knew we couldn't keep this up forever. I needed to find a way to end this insanity before any of us sustained serious injuries -- or worse. Then the mayor did me the biggest favor ever.

"Retreat!" Mayor Davis finally yelled. "Get out of here, you worthless cowards!"

His men fled, leaving behind a scene of carnage and destruction. Our clubhouse was in shambles, with broken furniture and shattered glass littering the floor. We were battered and bruised, but we'd won.

"Everyone okay?" Hatter asked, his voice hoarse from shouting and exertion. My brothers nodded, their eyes filled with a mixture of relief and anger.

"Eliza," I said, turning to her as she stared at me, tears streaming down her face. "You're safe now."

I hurried to her side and pulled her into my arms. She crumpled against me, and I felt her tears soaking my shirt. She might have lived with a brute of a man, but this type of fight was probably not what she was used to.

"Thank you," she whispered, her voice trembling.

"We protect our own," I replied, feeling an unexpected pang of tenderness toward the frightened woman. "And that includes you."

"Listen up," Hatter called out, as he surveyed the damage around us. "We may have won this battle, but the war's far from over. Mayor Davis and Sheriff Holmes will keep coming at us, harder and stronger each time. We need to be ready."

"Damn right," Absolem agreed. "Let's clean this mess up and take a breather before we have to jump back into the thick of it."

"Underland MC stands strong," I declared, meeting each of my brothers' gazes in turn. "We won't let them tear us apart. We'll bring justice to those bastards -- together."

As we began to clean up the wreckage, I looked around the room and spotted Jo coming in from the kitchen. I urged Eliza to go to her and helped my brothers with the mess the fight had left behind. I'd have to talk to Eliza and come up with a plan for future events like this. If it happened again, I needed to know she was hidden somewhere safe.

* * *

The women were tucked into bed, and the rest of us were once more focused on what we needed to do next. There wouldn't be any rest or fun until we'd handled this problem.

"I'm here if anyone needs me or has questions, but like I've said before, Cheshire has point on this one. So I'll let him assign the tasks," Hatter said.

I scanned the room. "Knave, I need you to track down connections between Sheriff Holmes and any other criminal organizations he's tied to."

"The Pres and March, I need you two to investigate any properties or assets linked to Holmes.

There has to be something hidden that can help us build our case against him."

"Absolem, keep digging into his financial backers," I continued. Absolem nodded, his brow furrowed. He knew if we could track all the money, we might be able to cut off his finances and leave him hobbled.

"Lastly, Rabbit, you're going to use your skills to gather intel from the streets. We don't know who else might be involved with this scum, so we need ears everywhere."

"What about me?" Carpenter asked.

"I want you to work with Jo and Eliza on some self-defense and find them places to hide if something like today's fight happens again. I think we'll all be able to focus more if we know they're safe."

"On it," he said.

"And me?" Mock asked.

"I need you to rotate through everyone with a specific task and help as needed." Mock gave me a brisk nod.

"Am I chopped liver?" Tweedle asked. "Makes me think I'm fucking useless or something."

"I want you on standby to watch over the women. I can't think of a more important task," I said.

"Fine." Tweedle looked aggravated, but I could tell my words had pleased him.

"Let's get to it!" I commanded, and the room erupted in action.

As we split up and set our plan in motion, I could feel the tension in the air. We were walking a dangerous tightrope, navigating a treacherous world of underground crime and corruption. One misstep could cost us everything.

* * *

I could feel my heart pounding in my chest as I slipped into the darkened office of one of Holmes' associates, rifling through drawers and files for any incriminating information. The acrid scent of stale cigar smoke hung heavy in the air.

"Got something," Rabbit whispered into my earpiece, his voice barely audible above the hum of traffic outside. "Just spotted a meeting between some of Holmes' men and a couple of guys from out of town. Looks like they're making a deal. I can't be one hundred percent sure, but it looked like cash was handed off."

"Stay on them," I ordered, my fingers gripping the edge of the desk as I strained to hear any noise that might signal someone approaching. "We need to know who we're up against, aside from the locals."

"Understood," he replied.

There was no room for mistakes, no chance for second-guessing. We were all in this together, each member of the Underland MC playing their part in the fight for justice. And as we delved deeper into the shadows, uncovering the depths of Sheriff Holmes' criminal empire, I knew we were inching closer to our goal -- and there would be no turning back.

* * *

As the night drew on, our efforts began to bear fruit. The intel we'd gathered painted a picture darker than any of us had anticipated. Huddled together around the kitchen table, I shared our findings with the team.

"Sheriff Holmes has been running this sick operation for years," I said, fury filling me at all the rotten things he'd gotten away with. "He's got his filthy hands in every corner of this town, and it's time we put an end to it."

Absolem nodded. "We can't let that bastard get away with this any longer."

"We've got the upper hand now. We just need to play it smart," Knave said.

I nodded, my mind racing with possibilities. "We need to gather more evidence, and then we'll bring him down -- hard. We can't turn him in to the law since he *is* the law. Which means we'll have to get justice our own way."

Rabbit was the only one not here. He was still tailing the sheriff and the men from out of town. My earpiece buzzed with an incoming call, and I connected it.

"Cheshire," Rabbit's voice whispered through my earpiece, urgency lacing every word. "You need to see this."

"Talk to me," I replied, my heart pounding in my chest as I braced myself for whatever revelation awaited.

"Found some sort of ledger," he said, the faint rustle of paper filling my ears. "Names, dates, amounts... It's all here, man. This is the key."

"Bring it back," I instructed, my breath catching in my throat as the implications of his discovery sunk in. "This could be the break we've been waiting for."

"Got it," Rabbit responded.

I ended the call and looked at my brothers. "Rabbit found what we need. We're one step closer to bringing those assholes down."

Chapter Eight

Eliza

I flipped through the dog-eared pages of a book, losing myself in the gritty story. I'd been gifted several, but this had been my favorite so far. For a few blissful moments, I wasn't in that shithole anymore. I was somewhere else, living a different life. Although, technically, I really had found my freedom thanks to the Underland MC. But as long as my father was out there, I knew there was a chance I'd end up right back in hell.

A gentle knock made me jump. Jo appeared in the doorway, a smile on her face. She was holding a tray with two steaming mugs. "Hey. Thought you could use some tea." Jo set the tray on the table next to me and took a seat, her movements careful and slow like she was trying not to spook a wild animal.

I eyed the mug suspiciously. People didn't do nice things for nothing. There was always a catch. But the tea smelled good, comforting.

"Thanks," I muttered, picking up the mug and letting the warmth seep into my hands. I took a sip, the hot liquid soothing my raw throat. When was the last time someone made me tea? Probably when my mom had been alive. I knew she'd enjoyed one that smelled of cinnamon.

Jo sat there in silence, sipping her own mug. She wasn't pushing, not prying. Just... being there. It was strange. But also kind of nice?

I glanced over at her, noticing the signs of someone who'd fought their own battles. She may not wear bruises anymore, but her posture, the way she seemed aware of her surroundings, told me she'd once feared someone or something. We'd talked a little, so I knew she didn't have the most spectacular past, but I also didn't know the details.

Maybe that's why I didn't feel the need to run her off or throw up my walls. Because in a messed-up way, I felt like she got it. Got me.

I went back to my book, the pages more battered than ever. Normally, I'd never fold down a page, but this one had already been damaged when I got it. No matter how long I stared at the page, I didn't really see the words anymore. My mind churned, an unfamiliar feeling taking root in my gut.

Was this what safety felt like? Acceptance? I was almost afraid to trust it. After living in fear for so long, I didn't know how I was supposed to feel or how I should act. Everyone here had been nice to me, and genuinely seemed kind. But I knew my father showed one face to the world and another to me. It left me questioning everyone I met, wondering how much of what I saw was the real them and how much was them playing a part.

For now, I'd let myself breathe. Let myself just exist in this quiet moment, broken but not shattered. And for the first time in forever, I didn't feel quite so alone.

Jo's voice broke the silence, her words hesitant. "That book you were reading... was it any good?"

I blinked, surprised she'd even asked. People usually didn't care what I was into. Of course, I'd mostly been staring at it, attempting to read. This time, anyway. I had read the story before, so I already knew what happened. "It was good, probably my favorite of the ones I was given." I ran my finger along the dog-eared pages. "Helped me escape, you know? My mind feels like it's running non-stop, so reading lets me take a break from life."

She nodded, a flicker of understanding in her eyes. "I get that. Books were my lifeline growing up. Still are." She took another sip of tea, lost in thought for a moment. "Who's your favorite author?"

I chewed on my lip, not used to talking about this stuff. But something about Jo made me want to open up, just a little. "I don't really have a favorite author, but I do love books about haunted houses. Not non-fiction, but the horror type, where unseen beings can wreak havoc, or even end lives."

A smile tugged at the corner of her mouth. "I'm more into romance and mystery myself. I guess I felt like I was living in a horror movie long enough I didn't really get into the genre. But I do enjoy a good ghost story around Halloween."

We fell into an easy conversation, swapping book recommendations and favorite quotes. It was surreal, connecting with someone like this. Like maybe we weren't so different after all. The way she'd talked about her life made me think we were similar in many ways, but I wasn't going to pry. If she wanted to tell me about her past, I'd wait for her to offer the story and not try to drag it out of her.

As the tea dwindled in our mugs, Jo shifted gears. "You know, art was a lifesaver for me. Painting, specifically." She ran a finger over a faded scar on her wrist, lost in a memory. "It helped me process the darkness, turn it into something beautiful. Now I mostly sketch. The club loaded me up with art supplies. Rabbit likes to draw too."

I swallowed hard, my own scars itching beneath my sleeves. "I used to sketch," I admitted quietly, the words rusty from disuse. "Before everything went to hell. Sometimes even afterward I would. My dad hated it. Every time he found one of my sketch pads, he'd destroy it."

Jo's eyes met mine, a flicker of hope sparking in their depths. "You should try it again sometime. It's never too late to reclaim that part of yourself."

Her words hit me like a sucker punch, knocking the air from my lungs. Could I really pick up a pencil again, after all this time? What if I wasn't any good now?

The idea terrified me. But it also ignited a tiny ember in my chest, one I thought had long since burned out. It made me wonder if there was still a glimmer of light left in me after all.

"Want to try?" she asked.

"What if I suck at it now?"

She shrugged. "You won't know if you don't attempt to draw anything. And so what if it's not the greatest? What matters is how it makes you feel."

I nodded. "All right, but I don't have anything."

"Wait here." She fled from the room and returned a few minutes later with a stack of sketchbooks and a box of pencils. "Mind if I draw too?"

"Sure." I smiled. This could be fun, and perhaps it would make me reconnect with the part of myself I'd lost somewhere along the way.

She handed me a brand-new sketch pad and I took one of the pencils. Sitting at an angle where she couldn't see the pad, I started drawing. I didn't know how long we sat there, but by the time Jo said anything, I'd filled quite a few pages.

"May I?" Her voice was undemanding.

I hesitated, fear and doubt swirling inside me. But Jo's gentle gaze steadied me. I nodded.

Carefully, she took the sketchbook, handling it like it was something precious. She settled beside me, the warmth of her body soaking into my skin, chasing away the chill that had seeped into my bones.

Slowly, reverently, she opened the cover. A small gasp escaped her lips as she took in the first drawing. It was a self-portrait, raw and unflinching. Every scar, every bruise laid bare on the page.

"Oh, Eliza," she breathed. "This… this is incredible. The emotion, the honesty… it's stunning."

I ducked my head, unused to such praise. "It's nothing special," I mumbled. "Just some scribblings."

Jo shook her head firmly. "No, it's not nothing. It's everything. This is your truth, your story. And it deserves to be seen, to be celebrated."

She continued to flip through the pages, each one a window into my shattered soul. A landscape of jagged edges and bleeding skies. A portrait of a broken girl with haunted eyes. An abstract explosion of rage.

"You have such a gift," Jo marveled. "The way you captured pain, resilience, hope… it's breathtaking. You need to keep doing this, Eliza. Keep creating, keep expressing yourself. The world needs your art."

Tears pricked at my eyes, blurring the pages. No one had ever believed in me like that before. Seen me, truly seen me, and thought I was worth something.

"You really think so?" I whispered, hardly daring to hope.

Jo reached out, took my hand in hers. Her skin was warm, her grip strong and sure. "I know so," she said firmly. "You're a survivor, Eliza. A fighter. And your art… it's a testament to that. Never stop believing in yourself. Because I never will. And I know the men here will always believe in you too."

Something inside me cracked open at her words. I felt raw, exposed, like she had peeled back my skin and glimpsed the fragile heart beneath.

I took a shuddering breath, then began to speak.

"This one," I said, pointing to the sketch of a girl curled in on herself, "I drew this while thinking about the first time he broke my ribs. I thought I was going to die that night. Thought that was it, you know? But I survived. This is the first time I've been able to purge some of that pain, pouring it all out onto the page."

Jo listened intently, her thumb rubbing soothing circles on my palm. It grounded me, anchored me, gave me the courage to keep going.

"And this," I continued, flipping to the landscape, "I drew this while thinking about the day I left him. The day I finally broke free. It felt like... like I was being reborn, and at the same time I was terrified. Scared he'd catch me. Worried the Underland MC wouldn't be as helpful as I'd been told."

Jo nodded, her eyes shining with understanding. "I know that feeling," she murmured. "That moment when you realize you're stronger than you ever thought possible. That you survived the unsurvivable."

"Is that a word?" I asked.

She smiled faintly. "Probably not, but I'm making it one."

Her words wrapped around me like a blanket, warm and comforting. For the first time in what felt like forever, I didn't feel alone. I didn't feel like a freak, a broken thing.

I felt seen. Understood. Accepted.

Jo's hand tightened around mine, a lifeline in the darkness. "You are amazing, Eliza," she said. "Your strength, your resilience... it's inspiring. You've been through hell, but you're still standing. Still fighting. And that's incredible. Not everyone can break free."

I leaned into her touch, soaking up her warmth, her steadiness. The hole in my chest, the one that had been aching for so long... it felt a little less empty now. A little less raw.

For the first time in what felt like forever, I felt the beginnings of something that might have been healing.

Jo glanced at the sketchbook again, a glimmer of an idea dancing in her eyes. "You know," she said slowly, "I've been working on some poetry lately. Trying to put my own demons into words." She hesitated, then plunged ahead. "What if... what if we combined your drawings with my poems? We could create something beautiful out of all this ugliness. And if we can come up with enough pages, maybe we could find a way to have it published? There have to be more women out there who can relate to what we've been through, who need to know it's possible to break free."

My heart skipped a beat, a thrill of excitement rushing through me. "You mean... like a collaboration?"

Jo grinned, her whole face lighting up. "Exactly. We could tell our stories, Eliza. Show the world that we're more than just victims."

The idea took root, blossoming into possibility. I imagined our pain, our healing, our hopes, all woven together. A tapestry of trauma and triumph.

"I love it," I breathed, my fingers already itching for a pencil. "Let's do it."

While I sketched for another few hours, she sorted through her poems, and it looked like she might even be writing more of them. When I set the book and pencil down, she pulled it over.

"This one," she murmured, tapping a charcoal sketch of a woman emerging from a cage. "I have a poem that fits it perfectly."

She flipped through her notebook until she

found the poem she sought. Her voice was soft as she
read it to me.

> *Trapped in a cage,*
> *Bars forged in fear and hatred.*
> *Imprisoned.*
> *Broken.*
> *But I'm the key.*
> *And today,*
> *I choose to be free.*

A lump rose in my throat, tears stinging my eyes.
Jo's words, my art… it was like they were made for
each other. Like we were meant to become friends.

We lost ourselves in the creative process, Jo's
words danced across the pages as I brought them to
life with bold strokes of my pencil. The outside world
faded away until there was nothing but the two of us,
our art, and the unspoken bond that had grown
stronger with each passing minute.

Laughter bubbled up from some forgotten place
inside me as Jo cracked a joke, her eyes sparkling with
mischief. It felt strange, foreign, like my body didn't
quite remember how to make the sound. But it also felt
right. Like I was remembering how to live again.

"I can't believe I actually had fun," I admitted,
the words tumbling out before I could stop them. "I
didn't think I ever would again, after…"

I trailed off, the ghosts of my past rising up to
choke me. But Jo just nodded, her gaze filled with
understanding.

"I know," she murmured, her hand finding mine.
"But we are more than what they did to us, Eliza. We
aren't just survivors. We're fighters. Artists. And we
can show the world just how strong we are."

Her words ignited a fire in my chest, a blaze of

determination that consumed the lingering shadows. I squeezed her hand.

"Together," I whispered, and it was a promise. A vow. "We can do it together."

I never thought I'd find solace in another person again, not after the hell I had endured. Trust was a luxury I couldn't afford, a weakness that could be exploited. But here, in this moment, with Jo by my side, I thought it might be okay to let people in. At least, the ones here at the clubhouse.

"I never knew words could be so powerful," I whispered, my voice raw with emotion as I traced the lines of Jo's poetry with a reverent finger. "The way you wove them together, it was like…"

"Magic?" Jo finished, her lips curving into a smile that was tinged with sadness. "Yeah, I used to think so too. Before… I mean, I guess I haven't thought about it much since I picked it back up. It was just a way to process everything in my head."

She didn't need to say more. We both knew the horrors that haunted our pasts, the scars that marred our souls.

She cleared her throat. "As I said before, I draw too. Actually, I only started writing poems again recently. Like you, I worried I wouldn't be good at it anymore."

For so long, I'd believed I was worthless, that my existence held no value beyond what my abuser decided. But here, with Jo, I was beginning to see the truth: I was an artist. A creator. A survivor.

As I finished my last drawing, the final lines taking shape on the page, a sense of peace settled over me, a balm to the jagged edges of my shattered heart. Jo's presence was a steady anchor, a reminder that I was not alone in this fight.

We were warriors. We were healers. We were artists. And together, we had risen from the ashes of our pasts, and we were going to paint the world anew.

Chapter Nine

Cheshire

I slid into the booth across from Park. He eyed me, suspicious. Smart man. I let him stew a minute while I sipped my black coffee. The diner bustled around us, clanking silverware and sizzling grease. Finally, I leaned in.

"We needed to talk. Sheriff Holmes wasn't the only rotten apple in this barrel of pigs. Mayor Davis and Robert Lewis -- they were in on it too." I watched his face, waiting for the info to sink in.

Park blinked. Furrowed his brow. "What? No way. You sure about this?" He gripped his mug tighter, knuckles going white.

I nodded, holding his gaze. "Dead sure. We need to root out the whole infestation before this town turns to total shit."

Park sat back heavily, processing. I could practically see the gears turning behind those green eyes. Poor bastard, still wanted to believe in the system. Well, time for a wake-up call.

"Sheriff Holmes was just the start," I pressed on. "We're talking high-level fuckery here. Real deep. Your precious boys in blue couldn't handle this. Not to mention, most are looking the other way if not outright helping."

Park glared at me, jaw clenched. For a second I thought he might take a swing. But then something shifted. A hardness settled over his face.

"All right. I'm in," he said.

I smiled, cold and sharp. *Welcome to the real world, Deputy. Time to get your hands dirty.*

"I just... I don't understand how this can be happening." He ran his hands through his hair, staring into his cup of coffee like it had all the answers.

He glanced up, his gaze finding mine, almost as if he was hoping I'd tell him it had all been a lie. I wanted to reassure him, tell him everything would be fine. But truthfully, I wasn't sure how we'd fare this time. Eddie Lewis had been one thing, but this… this was so much bigger.

"Everything I've believed in, fought for… it was all a crock of shit. I refuse to stand by and let it happen," Park said.

I stared at him, waiting for him to confirm he'd join us. If he decided not to, then I'd walk away and pretend we never had this talk.

Park firmed his jaw. "Whatever it takes to clean up this mess. Just point me in the right direction."

I smiled in answer. I'd hoped he would join our cause. We needed one good man in law enforcement in this place. Once we got rid of the corruption, someone would need to step in as the new sheriff, and I had a feeling Park would fill those shoes nicely. Even though he'd have to run for office and be elected, I had no doubt he'd win, as long as we killed the corruption in town. Hell, I'd help with his campaign if I needed to.

Park drained his coffee and dropped some money on the table. "This one's on me. Call me when you're ready for me."

"Why don't you come with me?" I asked. "Better to be in on this every step of the way, right?"

"Fine."

I stood and we went outside. I climbed onto my bike and started her up. As I backed out of the space, I saw Park pulling out in his truck a few spots away. With a wave of my hand, I motioned for him to follow me.

I led Park through the nearly empty streets. The

clubhouse loomed ahead, and I pulled through the gates, parking out front. I killed the engine and swung off, my boots hitting the pavement.

Glancing over at Park, I saw the determination etched into his features. Good. He'd need it.

"Fair warning," I muttered as we approached the door. "The boys might not roll out the welcome mat for you. Hard to know who to trust these days. And since you're a deputy…"

Park nodded, jaw tight. "I get it. I'll win them over."

I snorted. Easier said than done. But hey, maybe he'd surprise me. I'd already given Hatter a heads-up as to what I was doing, so at least the president wouldn't be surprised.

I shoved open the door and stepped inside. Home, sweet home.

Conversation died as we entered. All eyes locked onto Park, suspicion and hostility radiating from every corner. I felt him tense beside me, but to his credit, he didn't flinch. Anyone who'd seen him around town in uniform knew he was part of the Warren Sheriff's Department.

Mock leaned against the bar, arms crossed over his broad chest. "The hell's this, Cheshire? Since when do we let badges in here?"

I flashed him a grin, all teeth. "Since they started playing for our team. Park's here to help."

Tweedle scoffed from his perch on the couch. "Help? We don't need his kind of help."

The others muttered their agreement, edging closer. Park stood his ground, chin high. I had to admit, the man had balls.

"Look," he said, voice steady. "I know you don't trust me. I get it. But this is my town too. And I'll be damned if I let it burn while I sit on my ass and watch."

The brothers exchanged glances, considering. It was a start. It wouldn't take them long to realize why I'd brought him.

"So," I drawled, slinging an arm around Park's shoulders. He stiffened but didn't shrug me off. "What do you say, boys? Ready to raise a little hell and take back our streets?"

A beat of silence. Then, slowly, nods all around.

"Fine. But I've got my eye on you," Tweedle said, glaring at Park.

Park met his gaze unflinching. "Likewise."

I clapped my hands, grin stretching wide. *Oh, this is gonna be fun.* "All right, then. Let's get to work."

Out of the corner of my eye, I caught Jo and Eliza slipping away from the kitchen, heading down the hall. Smart girls, steering clear of the pissing contest.

I turned back to Park, jerking my chin toward the door. "Walk with me."

We stepped outside, the cool night air a welcome relief from the tension inside. I lit a cigarette, took a deep drag.

"You sure about this, Deputy? Once you cross that line, there's no going back. What you've done so far isn't as bad as what's coming. You've bent the law. That's completely different from annihilating it."

Park's jaw clenched. "I've never been more sure of anything in my life. I took an oath to protect and serve, and that's exactly what I intend to do. Even if it means I have to throw the rulebook out the window. Blindly following someone like Sheriff Holmes isn't the right thing to do."

I nodded, blowing out a stream of smoke. "Bending, breaking… it's all the same in the end. Just don't lose yourself in the process."

"I won't," he said firmly. "I know what I'm fighting for. A safe town, a place where people can live without fear. That's worth any price."

I studied him for a long moment, searching for any hint of doubt or hesitation. There was none. Just steely resolve and a fire in his eyes that matched my own.

"All right, then," I said, flicking away my cigarette. "Let's do this. But fair warning, it's going to get ugly before it gets better."

Park's lips quirked in a humorless smile. "I'm counting on it."

We headed back inside, with Deputy Park ready to face whatever hell awaited us.

Inside the clubhouse, the air was thick with tension. Tweedle and Mock were waiting, arms crossed, suspicion etched into every line of their faces. I didn't think Park would win them over very quickly, but in time, they'd realize this was the right move. I'd never have brought him here otherwise.

"You two better remember I vouched for him. That should be enough for anyone here. And Hatter gave him permission to be here," I said.

Mock scoffed, his gaze darting between us. "Vouched for him? What, because he says he wants to help? Words are cheap, man. We need more than that."

I took a step forward, squaring my shoulders. "We need all the help we can get, and you know it. This isn't about the club. It's the entire damn town. Not to mention, Park has already stepped up to lend a hand once. He's assured me he's on board no matter the risk."

Tweedle's scowl deepened, but I could see a flicker of understanding in his eyes. He knew I was right, even if he didn't want to admit it.

"Park here is a *good* deputy. He's one of the few left in this Godforsaken place. If he says he's in, then he's in. End of story. I'm not going to make him sit on the sidelines." Mock opened his mouth to argue, but I cut him off with a sharp look. "We're all on the same side here, fighting the same battle. We can't afford to be divided, not now."

Silence fell, heavy and tense. I could practically hear the gears turning in their heads, weighing the risks against the potential rewards. I'd meant what I said. If I thought Park would do anything to hurt the club, I'd have never brought him here. It wasn't like we were running guns or drugs, or doing anything illegal. Although, if I thought the best way to handle Holmes was to put him six feet under, I wouldn't hesitate.

Finally, Tweedle nodded, a single, sharp jerk of his head. "Fine. But if this goes sideways, just remember I said I didn't trust him."

I met his gaze steadily, unflinching. "I'm willing to bet Park will make you eat those words."

Mock said nothing, but the set of his jaw told me he wasn't happy about this. Tough shit. We had bigger problems to worry about than his delicate sensibilities.

I turned to Park, clapping him on the shoulder. "Welcome to the fight, Deputy. Let's hope you're ready for it. Something tells me this is going to get real ugly."

He met my gaze, and there was no fear in his eyes. Only determination and a fierce, unshakable resolve.

"I'm ready," he said simply. "Let's bring these bastards down."

And just like that, the deal was sealed. *No going back now. God help us all.*

"First things first, we need to figure out our next

move. Sheriff Holmes isn't going to go down without a fight."

Park leaned in, his voice low and urgent. "I've been thinking about that. If we could get some hard evidence of his involvement in the trafficking ring, something that tied him directly to it... Maybe the Feds would step in?"

"First off, we've already found some women who he'd grabbed in order to sell them. Not sure there's more damning proof than that. But... even if it was enough to take him down, the man has more layers of protection than a fucking onion. I have a feeling he has ties outside of Warren, so going to the FBI or anyone else would be risky."

Park's brow furrowed, his green eyes intense. "What about Eliza? His daughter. Is she safe? Should we get her out of there?"

The question caught me off-guard, and for a moment, I wasn't sure how to respond. I hadn't expected him to ask about her, not here, not now. What connection did Park have with Eliza? And how the fuck did he know her? I'd thought the sheriff kept her under lock and key.

"She's as safe as she can be," I said finally, choosing my words carefully. "We already got her away from the sheriff. How come you don't know that?"

Park paused. "What do you mean?"

"Is the sheriff not actively searching for her? Has no one noticed she's missing?" I asked. "Wait... she said something about him telling everyone she's sick, and she was even homeschooled. So has anyone in town seen her before?"

There was a flicker of something in his eyes that I couldn't quite read. Concern, maybe. Or something else entirely.

"Um, no. As far as I know, no one has really seen her. Not since she was just a little kid. Once her mom died, everything changed. As for how I know about her, I've met her a few times at the sheriff's house."

I clenched my hands into fists. "You've met her but never thought something was off? Why the hell has she been abused all this time?"

"I never saw signs of him hitting her," Park said. "If I had… Honestly, I'm not sure I could have done anything. One deputy against the entire Sheriff's Department? But for what it's worth, I'm really glad she's safe."

An uncomfortable silence stretched between us, heavy with unspoken words and unanswered questions. I cleared my throat, eager to move on. The way he looked when he talked about her… I didn't like it. I had to wonder if Park had feelings for Eliza.

"We need to be smart about this," I said, steering the conversation back to the task at hand. "Holmes is a slippery bastard, and he has eyes and ears everywhere. We can't afford to make any mistakes. After we freed those girls before, he probably locked down his operation pretty tight. It's what I would do. So getting to him won't be easy."

Park nodded, his jaw set with determination. "I'll do whatever it takes. This ends now."

"Damn right it does," I said. "Let's get to work."

As Park and I had headed out of the clubhouse, the cool night air hit my face like a slap. I lit up a cigarette, taking a long drag before exhaling slowly.

"I wish I'd known about Eliza's situation sooner," Park said suddenly, his voice low and full of regret. "I don't know how I could've helped her or gotten her out of there before things got so bad. Just the same, maybe I could have thought of something. Knowing she's been suffering all this time... Man, that hurts my heart."

I narrowed my eyes at him, not liking where this conversation was going. "Eliza isn't your business, Deputy. You focus on taking down Holmes and let us worry about her."

Park shook his head, frustration etched into every line of his face. "You don't understand. The entire town believed him when he said Eliza was too sick to leave the house. He hid her away, and we all bought it like a bunch of fucking idiots."

I took another drag of my cigarette, considering his words. It wasn't surprising that Holmes would pull some shit like that, but it still made my blood boil.

"Well, now you know the truth," I said finally, flicking ash onto the pavement. "And you're going to help us make that bastard pay for what he's done."

Park nodded, his eyes hard with determination. "Damn right, I will."

We shook hands, a silent agreement passing between us. As I watched him walk away, disappearing into the shadows of the night, I couldn't help but wonder what Eliza was going to do when all this was over.

Her old man was a piece of shit, but he was still her father. And if the club ended up putting a bullet in his head, that was going to leave a mark no amount of time or therapy could erase.

I sighed heavily, crushing my cigarette beneath the heel of my boot. It was a fucked-up situation, no matter how you sliced it. But at the end of the day, family was family. And the Underland MC took care of its own. Now that Eliza was here with us, she was one of ours too.

And I was starting to hope she'd be mine.

I stuffed my hands in my pockets and had headed off to find Eliza, my mind already racing with plans and possibilities. Once the dust settled and she was free of her father, would she be willing to stay here with me?

Chapter Ten

Eliza

I watched Cheshire from across the clubhouse, my heart pounding. He was talking with some of the other Underland MC members, that sly grin on his face as always. Every time I saw him, my stomach did flips. Suddenly, his piercing blue eyes locked onto mine. Shit, he'd caught me staring. A mischievous smirk spread across his face, and my cheeks went hot. Embarrassment and excitement coursed through me at the same time.

Cheshire said something to the guys and strolled over to me, his swagger oozing confidence. "See something you like, doll?" he asked, raising an eyebrow.

"I… um…" The words got stuck in my throat. *Get it together, Eliza. Don't let him fluster you.*

He leaned in close, his breath hot on my ear. "Cat got your tongue? Or do I just have that effect on you?"

My face burned even hotter, but I forced myself to meet his penetrating gaze. Those damn blue eyes saw right into my soul. I was drawn to Cheshire like a moth to flame, even though I knew I might get burned.

I took a deep breath, steeling my nerves. "Can we talk somewhere more… private?" I managed to say, my voice barely above a whisper.

Cheshire's eyes flashed with intrigue. "Lead the way, doll."

He gestured for me to go first, that infuriating smirk still plastered on his handsome face. Weaving through the room of rowdy bikers, I made my way to a quieter corner of the clubhouse. The bass from the music pulsed through the floor, matching my racing heartbeat.

Once we were alone, I turned to face Cheshire, my hands fidgeting anxiously at my sides. "Look, I…" God, why was this so hard? "I thought you were…"

"Devilishly handsome? Wickedly charming?" He grinned, stepping closer. "Tell me something I don't know, sweetheart."

I rolled my eyes, even as a smile tugged at my lips. "You're impossible."

"And you love it." His voice dropped an octave, sending shivers down my spine.

He was right. As much as Cheshire frustrated me, I couldn't resist his magnetic pull. The way he looked at me, like he could read my every thought… It was unnerving and thrilling all at once.

I opened my mouth to reply, but the words died on my tongue as Cheshire reached out, tucking a stray lock of hair behind my ear. His touch lingered, rough fingertips grazing my skin. "What's on your mind, Eliza?" he murmured, blue eyes searching mine. "Tell me what you want."

My pulse raced under his intense gaze. What did I want? I wanted him, all of him, but admitting that out loud terrified me. Even admitting to myself was scary. I'd never known the kind touch of a man. Never dated. I had a feeling Cheshire was far more than I'd be able to handle, and yet… I still wanted to try.

"I…" My voice trembled. "I couldn't stop thinking about you, Cheshire."

"Is that so?" He leaned in closer. "Glad to know I'm not the only one."

I shivered, equal parts aroused and unnerved by his proximity. "What are you saying?"

"C'mon, doll, don't play coy." Cheshire pulled back just enough to meet my eyes. "You feel this thing between us. The tension. The heat. I've seen it in your eyes when you watch me. Can feel it in the air around us."

He wasn't wrong. Every interaction with Cheshire was charged, electric, like a live wire ready to spark. It was exhilarating and scary as hell.

"Maybe I did," I whispered, emboldened by his admission. "But what do we do about it? I've never... I mean..."

Cheshire gripped my hip, his touch searing through the denim fabric. "Oh, I have a few ideas."

His voice was low, laced with sinful promise. My brain short-circuited, desire clouding rational thought. I knew falling for Cheshire was a risk, but with every word, every touch, I found myself caring less about the consequences. I'd already survived so much. Was it wrong to want to live a little? To experience things other women my age had already done?

His lips hovered a hairsbreadth from mine, his eyes dark with want. "Tell me to stop, Eliza," he murmured. "Tell me you don't want this."

I couldn't. I wouldn't.

"Don't stop," I breathed, closing the distance between us.

Our lips met in a searing kiss, hungry and desperate. Cheshire's hands roamed my body, leaving trails of fire in their wake. I arched into his touch, craving more.

He backed me up until I was pressed against the wall, his body a solid line of heat against mine. His lips left my mouth to blaze a path along my jaw, down my neck. Despite the aches I still felt, I didn't want him to stop. If I brought it up now, I knew he'd back off, and that was the last thing I wanted.

"Fuck, Eliza," he groaned against my skin. "You drive me crazy."

I tangled my fingers in his hair, holding him close. "The feeling is mutual. It doesn't make sense. I should be terrified of you, of the feelings I have when I'm around you. But for some reason, I trust you not to hurt me."

Cheshire nipped at my pulse point, drawing a gasp from my lips. His hands skimmed down my sides, toying with the hem of my shirt.

A distant *crash* from the main room of the clubhouse broke through the haze of lust. Cheshire pulled back, his breathing ragged.

"We should have taken this somewhere else," he said, his voice rough with desire.

I nodded, not trusting myself to speak. Cheshire took my hand, lacing our fingers together, and led me down a dimly lit hallway. I wasn't sure where we were going, and I didn't care right then. I just wanted more time with him.

He stopped outside one of the bedroom doors, turned the knob, and pushed it open. Inside lay a small, Spartan room.

Cheshire pulled me inside, kicking the door shut behind us. In an instant, his lips were back on mine, his hands sliding beneath my shirt to caress the bare skin on my back.

I lost myself in his touch, in the feel of his body against mine. Fears and doubts faded away, replaced by pure, unadulterated want. Nothing else mattered except this moment, except this man, even though I might regret my decision in the morning.

"Are you sure, Eliza?" he asked, his voice rough and low.

"Yes. I want more."

One corner of his lips tipped up. "I have a feeling you don't even know what you're asking for. Am I right?"

"If you're asking if I've kissed anyone before, or gone on dates, then the answer is no. My father wouldn't allow it." I stared up at him. Was he going to tell me to leave? Had I ruined the moment?

"Then if I do anything you don't like, or you get scared, just tell me. I'll stop whenever you want me to." His gaze held mine and I nodded.

"I won't hurt you, doll." His voice was husky, and he leaned in.

My heart pounded in my chest as I whispered, "I trust you."

That seemed to be all the answer Cheshire needed. He pulled me closer, and our lips met again in a searing kiss, full of urgency and barely restrained passion. His hands roamed my body, setting every inch of me ablaze. He was rough but careful, every touch calculated to drive me insane with desire.

I'd never felt anything like it before. I clung to him, losing myself to the pleasure of his lips on mine.

Without breaking the kiss, he lifted me off my feet. I instinctively wrapped my legs around his waist as he carried me toward the bed. Setting me down gently, he hovered over me, his blue eyes intense as they raked over me.

"What is it?" I asked breathlessly.

"You're beautiful," he said simply. "More than you know."

My heart swelled at his words. I reached up to touch his cheek, then traced the lines of his tattoos that peeked out from under his shirt sleeve. There was so much I wanted to explore, to discover about this man who had so swiftly captured my heart.

He caught my hand and brought it to his lips, pressing a soft kiss against my knuckles. "Eliza," he murmured against my skin, sending shivers down my spine.

"Cheshire…" My voice was barely a whisper.

"You can call me Charlie," he said.

Slowly, carefully, Cheshire undressed us both. Each piece of clothing that fell to the floor felt like another barrier removed between us. When we were both left bare, he studied me with an intensity that made my heart race and my body flush with heat. I nearly covered myself, my cheeks flushing. No one had seen me naked like this before. Was I doing the right thing? Should we stop and take a step back?

"You sure about this?" His voice was gruff with desire, but there was a vulnerability in his gaze that tugged at my heartstrings. Hearing those words, and realizing he'd meant it when he said I could stop whenever I wanted, gave me the courage to keep going.

"I've never been more sure about anything in my life," I admitted.

He leaned in to whisper in my ear, "Then let's see what trouble we can get into, doll."

The heat between us intensified as we gazed into each other's eyes. He pulled me closer, our bodies flush against one another. His hands traced down my spine, sending shivers of anticipation through me. I couldn't help but moan at the feel of his rough palms on my skin.

"You have no idea what you do to me," he whispered hoarsely in my ear.

He kissed his way down my neck, sucking and nipping gently as he went. My breath hitched in my throat as he reached the valley between my breasts. His fingers brushed against my hardened nipples, causing me to arch my back involuntarily.

"Please," I whimpered, needing more of his touch. I'd never realized something could feel so incredible.

He chuckled darkly against my skin, his gaze possessive as he stared down at me. "Now you're mine."

Cheshire grabbed my wrists and pinned them above my head. I felt a brief moment of panic, but reminded myself this man wouldn't hurt me. He'd saved me.

He leaned down and captured one of my nipples between his teeth, eliciting a moan of pure pleasure from deep within me.

"Oh, God..." I groaned as he started to suck harder, rolling the sensitive bud between his teeth.

His free hand traced slowly down my stomach, over the curve of my hip, and into the wetness between my legs. He teased me with two fingers for a moment before sliding them inside me with ease. I threw my head back with a cry of pleasure as he began to thrust his fingers in and out rhythmically.

I'd thought it would hurt, had expected pain, but all I felt was pure bliss.

"Yes... More..." I panted out between moans and gasps for air as he took me to heights of ecstasy I'd never experienced before.

He made me come multiple times before settling over me. The weight of his body pressed against me, and I parted my thighs wider.

He groaned and pressed his forehead to my shoulder. "Shit. I don't have condoms, Eliza. Haven't been with anyone in over a year so I haven't needed them."

I licked my lips, wondering what the odds were I'd end up pregnant my first time having sex. "Do we have to use one?"

He arched an eyebrow. "You realize how risky that is, right?"

"But it's not likely I'll get pregnant, right?"

"It's like playing Russian roulette, Eliza, and let me tell you right now… if I get you pregnant, then you're mine. Not just for right now, but for always. Do you understand?"

"You mean, you'd want to marry me?" I asked. I'd never considered getting married. With the life I'd had with my dad, I'd always thought I'd die before I got the chance to start a family of my own.

"Yeah. I'd marry you." He smoothed my hair back. "Is that something you'd want?"

"Maybe." I worried at my bottom lip for a moment. "I never thought I'd have the chance to be with anyone like this, much less get married and have kids."

He kissed me, slow and deep. "Then let's stop here for now. I don't want to force you into something you don't want. This is your first taste of freedom, Eliza."

I reached up to cup his cheek. "You're rather amazing, you know that?"

He lay beside me, and I cuddled against him, no longer feeling embarrassed over my nakedness. We stayed like that for hours until I dozed off, only to wake a while later with the sun rising.

"Eliza," he murmured, his voice low and drowsy.

"Hmm?"

"What happens now?"

I lifted my head to look at him. His blue eyes were serious as they met mine. It was a good question. What happened now? I didn't have all the answers, but

I knew one thing for certain.

"We figure it out," I told him. "Together. I know I want more time with you, more of what we shared last night."

"Then that's what we'll do." He kissed me and got out of bed. "Rest as long as you want to. I need to check in with everyone."

I watched him dress and leave, still feeling warm and content. His words played through my mind on repeat, his sincerity unmistakable.

Finally, I stood up, dressing and running my fingers through my hair. I opened the door, steeling myself for the chaos of the clubhouse. And right on cue, a hail of curses and the clatter of pool balls greeted my ears. But my attention was drawn to the bar, where March and Hatter were engaged in an intense staring contest over their cards. Rabbit sat nearby watching them.

Jo entered the room and joined me. "So, spill," she said, resting her chin on her hands. "What happened with you and Cheshire?"

My cheeks warmed and she gave me a knowing smile. I didn't have to say anything. She clearly already knew what happened. "I think I like him. I mean, really like him," I said.

"Yeah, I bet you do. Sometimes when the right person comes along, you just know." Jo pressed her shoulder against mine. "Just like I knew with Hatter."

Chapter Eleven

Cheshire

I was starting to second-guess my invitation to Park. The moment Eliza had walked into the room, he'd stared at her like some lovesick fool. All the warning bells that had gone off in my head when he talked about her before made perfect sense now. He might not have met her many times, but clearly, she'd made an impression, and the fucker was infatuated with her. I didn't like it. Not even a little.

"I was happy to hear you were safe, Eliza. I wish I'd known you needed help," Park said, holding her gaze.

She gave him a slight smile, and it made my gut twist. "Thank you, but you and I both know there's nothing you could have done. If my dad thought you weren't on his side, something bad could have happened to you."

Park audibly swallowed. "Better to me than you. I'm so sorry, Eliza."

She shook her head. "It's fine, Park. I don't blame you or anyone else, just my dad."

I decided enough was enough and wanted to end their conversation. The sight of Park practically drooling over her was pissing me the fuck off. I leaned forward on the rough-hewn kitchen table, my hands clasped in front of me as I scanned the group. Hatter had Jo tucked tight against his side, but he met my gaze and gave me a nod. The floor was mine.

"All right, listen up," I said, my voice a low rasp. "We made progress on this Sheriff Holmes shit. Dug up some intel that connected the dots between the missing girls, suspicious money moving around, and a couple of VIPs in his pocket -- Mayor Davis and Robert

Lewis, as far as those in Warren go. But he has more outside of town."

I paused, letting that sink in. Park, the deputy in our corner, leaned in. "How solid's this info, Cheshire?"

A wry grin tugged at my lips. "Solid as my right hook, brother. Got the paper trail to prove it. These assholes were thick as thieves, all working to keep Holmes' sick operation going and line their own pockets."

As I laid it all out, my mind raced, slotting the pieces into place. The puzzle was starting to take shape, ugly as it was. These girls were snatched up and sold off like fucking cattle. My blood boiled at the thought. We had to shut this shit down and bury these bastards, whatever it took.

I glanced at Eliza, her face pale and her eyes haunted. She was holding it together, but barely. My heart twisted. Her own damn father had not only harmed her but had been selling girls. I wanted to reach out, take her hand, tell her it would be okay. But not here, not now.

"If we were going to hand him over to the authorities, then we'd need to keep digging. But I think we can all agree this one is going to get messy. Park is already aware we're going to need to work outside the law, and he's on board."

Nods all around the table, jaws set and eyes flashing with purpose. Hatter met my gaze again, pride and trust shining in his eyes. I felt the weight of it settle on my shoulders, but I carried it gladly. For the club, for the girls, for justice.

Sheriff Holmes and his cronies wouldn't know what hit them. No matter how dirty my hands were when this was over, at least I'd be able to live with myself. Letting people like them not only continue to live but reside in this town wasn't something I could condone.

A folder lay open on the table. March had pulled some photos of missing girls, and he'd used camera feeds around town to show the sheriff and his men snatching them off the streets. Eliza reached for one.

Eliza's hand shook as she gripped the photograph, her knuckles turning white. "I can't… I can't believe he could do something so awful." Her voice cracked, barely above a whisper. "These girls, they were just kids. How could he…"

She trailed off, her eyes shimmering with unshed tears. The anguish on her face hit me like a punch to the gut. I wanted to pull her close, shield her from all this shit. But I knew she was stronger than that. Stronger than she realized.

I leaned forward, my voice low and intense. "Your old man is a real piece of work, no doubt about that. But we'll take him down, Eliza. Him and every other scumbag involved in this."

I spread out the documents on the table, jabbing my finger at the damning evidence. "It went deep. The sheriff has his hooks in everywhere -- deputies, politicians, businessmen. A whole Goddamn network of corruption, all working together to line their pockets with blood money. It starts in Warren, then fans out not only in this state, but also into North Carolina and Virginia."

Anger simmered in my veins as I laid it all out. The web of lies, the betrayals, the shattered lives left in their wake. It was a fucking tragedy, and it ended now.

"We have solid leads on their operation from locations and shipment schedules to key players. It's time to plan our final move. But when the sheriff goes down, we need to handle the mayor and Robert Lewis as well."

Jo snorted. "Of course, Eddie's father would be into this sick shit. Like father like son, I guess."

Hatter hugged her tight. "We'll get them all, sweetheart."

Eliza set the photograph down, her jaw clenched with determination. "Whatever it takes, I want in. I can't let my father destroy any more lives."

Pride swelled in my chest at her strength, her resilience. She had been through hell, but she was still fighting. And with the Underland MC at her back, she would come out on top. I'd make damn sure of it.

I nodded, my trademark grin spreading across my face. At this point, it was like a mask I wore, one I seldom took off. "Damn right, darlin'. We'll burn this whole fucking thing to the ground and dance on the ashes."

The room crackled with energy, a sense of purpose settling over us all. Sheriff Holmes and his cronies had no idea what was coming for them. But they'd find out just how far the Underland MC would go to protect the innocent and seek justice.

Watch out, you sick fucks. Because we're coming for you!

As the others filed out of the room, their voices fading down the hallway, I turned to Eliza. She was still sitting at the table, her hands clasped tightly in front of her. I could see the tension in her shoulders, the weight of everything she had learned bearing down on her.

I pulled out the chair next to her and sat, our knees almost touching. "Hey," I said, ducking my head to catch her eye. "You okay?"

She took a shaky breath, her gaze meeting mine.

There was pain there, and anger, but also a fierce determination that sent a thrill through me.

"I will be," she said, her voice steady despite the storm I knew was raging inside her. "When this is over, when my father and his monsters are dead and buried, I'll be okay."

I reached out, covering her hands with my own. Her skin was soft and warm. I couldn't deny the pull between us, the connection that had been growing since the moment we met.

"I'm going to make you a promise, Eliza," I said, my voice low and intense. "I will protect you, no matter what. I'll stand by your side and fight like hell to bring these bastards down. You're not alone in this. You've got me, and you've got the Underland MC. We take care of our own, and like it or not, you're one of us now."

Eliza's breath caught, her eyes widening as she stared at me. For a moment, the world fell away, and it was just the two of us, lost in each other's gaze. I saw the trust there, the faith she had in me, and it humbled me even as it filled me with a fierce protectiveness.

"Thank you, Cheshire," she whispered. "I know you'll keep your word."

I squeezed her hands, a silent promise, before releasing her and standing up. "Damn right, darlin'. I'm going to kick some ass, and make sure the monsters in this world will never touch you again."

As I reached the doorway, I felt the weight of Eliza's gaze on my back. It was like a physical thing, a tingle between my shoulder blades that made me pause and glance back at her over my shoulder. She was still sitting there, her hands clasped tightly in her lap, her eyes fixed on me with an intensity that took my breath away.

For a moment, our eyes locked, and I felt the electric spark that seemed to ignite whenever we were together. It was dangerous, I knew. I should have given her a wide berth. Let her have a relationship with someone far better than me. But I couldn't. I'd known from the beginning she was mine, and I couldn't let her go. I wondered what it would be like to lose myself in her, to forget about the rest of the world and just be two people, coming together in a moment of passion and need.

I shook my head, pushing the thought away. Now wasn't the time for distractions, no matter how tempting she might be. I had a job to do, and I'd be damned if I let anything get in the way... even my feelings for Eliza.

Giving her a final nod, I stepped out of the room, letting the door swing shut behind me. Regardless of my own turbulent emotions, I had a mission. For Eliza, for the girls in the photograph, for the club I had sworn loyalty to. I moved through the dimly lit hallway with purpose, my boots echoing on the concrete floor.

I found Hatter in his office, pouring over maps and notes scattered across his desk. The room was filled with the scent of old paper and whiskey.

"You got a minute?" I asked.

"What's up?" He leaned back in his chair, the leather creaking.

"I think we both know that this battle we have coming up could be the last one for any of us. There's never a guarantee we'll make it out alive."

He nodded. "I'm aware."

"If something happens to me, I need to know the club will watch over Eliza."

Hatter snorted. "As if you even have to ask. I also assume that if I ever die, y'all will take care of Jo."

"And your kid?" I asked.

He narrowed his eyes. "Who said Jo is pregnant?"

I smirked. "Jo did. But if it's any consolation, she said she told you first."

He groaned and closed his eyes. "Does everyone know?"

"Nope. She only told me and Rabbit. Said she was too excited to hold it in. I think she wanted you to make the official announcement."

Hatter rubbed his hands over his face. "And I will, once this nightmare is over. I don't need anyone more distracted than they already are."

"This thing with Eliza... I haven't made it official, but she seems to feel the same way. I'm trying to give her time and not push too hard too fast. After everything she's been through, well, I'm scared I'll run her off."

Hatter nodded. "I get it. She seems to be settling in nicely. She and Jo are getting along well. They're even talking about making a book together. Something about art and poems. As long as it makes them happy... but I'm worried they'll get discouraged when it comes time to find someone to publish it."

I hadn't known Eliza was doing that. It just showed there was still a lot we needed to talk about. I wanted to know everything about her. Not just the horrific parts of her past, but simple things like her favorite foods, what type of music she liked, if she had a favorite movie.

Hatter cracked a smile. "And that right there is the look that means you're toast. You're already in love with her."

"Maybe. I know I like her. A lot."

"You'll figure it out. Just make sure you tell her

once you do. Don't hold that shit back for any reason."

"Yes, Dad," I said, giving him a mock salute. He flipped me off and I laughed as I left his office.

We weren't going after the sheriff just yet. Until it was time, I needed to be with Eliza more, and learn everything I could about her. She was still in the kitchen when I went back in there, still at the table where I'd left her. She'd made a cup of tea and sipped at the steaming brew.

I poured myself a cup of coffee and gestured to the seat beside her. "Mind if I sit?"

"Go ahead." She gave me a slight smile. "Everything okay?"

"Yeah. It's quiet for the moment. Thought we could take some time to get to know one another better. If you're up for it," I said.

"Are we going to play twenty questions?"

I shook my head. "Nope. Although, I'm game if you are."

"Um, I'd rather not."

"Then why don't we start with you asking me something? Obviously, I can't discuss a lot of my military background, but I'll truthfully answer anything I can."

"All right." She took another swallow of her tea and set the cup down. "Then, how old were you when you joined the military?"

"Eighteen, almost nineteen. I'd signed up for college, went one semester, and decided it wasn't for me. So I dropped out and enlisted."

"How long were you in?" she asked.

"I was dishonorably discharged after several years of service. Hatter, March, Absolem, and Rabbit all knew me from those days, even though they were enlisted longer. We all felt a little lost, so... Underland

MC came into existence." I drank more of my coffee, staring into the cup. "I guess we were missing that sense of brotherhood we'd had. Absolem had some money he'd inherited from his family. He bought this land, had the clubhouse built, and we all moved to Warren."

"But the club has been here a while, right?" she asked.

"It has."

"So, you're how old?" She leaned in a little. "Are you robbing the cradle by being with me?"

I bit my lip so I wouldn't laugh. "Well, since I don't know how old *you* are, it's hard to say if I'm 'robbing the cradle' or not. But I'm thirty-one."

"I'm twenty," she said. "Does that bother you?"

"Should it? From what I can tell, even though you've led a sheltered life in some ways, the hell you've survived makes you older than the average twenty-year-old."

She nodded. "You're right. Most women my age are probably off enjoying college, or trying to figure out their lives. I guess in one sense I'm doing that too. Since I never thought I'd be free of my father, I never made plans or dared to really dream. Only thing I knew I wanted and thought I'd never have was a family of my own."

"Favorite movie?" I asked.

"My dad monitored what I watched, but I always liked the family movies about hope and resilience. Like *Cinderella*. I like the live action better, though. In the cartoon, the evil stepfamily looked ugly on the outside. In the live action, they're all pretty."

"Like your dad?" I asked. "He's a decent-looking guy and has most people fooled into thinking he's nice."

"Right. Exactly like that. I think that's why it resonated with me. What about you?"

I leaned in closer to whisper. "Don't you dare tell anyone, but I like *Top Gun*. But if the guys find out my favorite movie is about a naval aviator, I'll never hear the end of it."

She smiled. "I can keep your secret. I guess that means you weren't in the navy."

"Marines. Me, Hatter, March, Absolem, and Rabbit. Although, Rabbit and I started out in the army. Served two years before switching to the Marines." I drained my coffee cup. "These days, if you sign up for two years, then you're expected to be in the reserves for an additional two years."

"Favorite drink?" she asked, eyeing my cup. "Coffee?"

"Hmm. For non-alcoholic beverages, yes. When it comes to alcohol, I tend to stick with beer. But I've been known to drink the harder stuff. What about you?"

She tapped her cup. "I like hot tea, and for cold drinks I like sweet tea."

"Then I guess we know a little more about each other now." I reached over to pat her thigh. "We should do this every day."

"Maybe twice a day," she said.

"I'm game if you are." Leaning over, I kissed her cheek. "I need to go check in with everyone and see what's going on. Rest and relax for a bit."

"Thanks, Cheshire. For everything."

"Anytime, doll. Anytime."

Chapter Twelve

Eliza

I sat at the kitchen table with my thoughts swirling like a damn tornado. After my talk with Cheshire, my head had been a mess. While I loved the time I got to spend with him, I couldn't help but feel guilty over my newfound happiness.

My dad was a monster. He'd done unspeakable things. It felt like I should suffer and not feel excited about getting a chance to actually have a life. It made me wonder if something was wrong with me.

The kitchen door creaked open, and I glanced up. It was Rabbit, concern etched across his face as he saw me. He stepped closer, two sketch pads clutched in his hands.

"Eliza, thought I might find you here," he said. "I can see you have a lot on your mind."

I just nodded, not trusting my voice. Emotions clogged my throat.

Rabbit pulled out a chair and sat across from me. He slid a sketch pad my way. "Here. I know you already have one, but I thought you might need a new one. Sometimes putting pen to paper helps sort out the demons, and if you have a lot of them, you'll go through a lot of paper." His eyes were kind, understanding. "Art's saved my sanity more than once, and Jo says you're pretty good. Give it a try. Maybe it will help you sort out the chaos in your head."

I stared at the blank page, my fingers trembling as I picked up a pencil. Rabbit flipped open his own pad and started sketching, the pencil dancing across the page. He glanced up at me.

"Let it out, Eliza. Whatever is tearing you up inside. Art doesn't judge."

I pressed the pencil tip to the paper and took a shaky breath. It was time to face these demons head-on, one stroke at a time.

I drew a tentative line across the page, unsure at first. But as the pencil moved, I felt something stirring deep inside me. The emotions I'd been trying so damn hard to suppress came bubbling to the surface.

Rabbit's pencil scratched against his paper, the sound oddly soothing. He didn't push me to talk, just let me find my own rhythm.

My hand started moving faster, the lines growing bolder. I poured my confusion, my guilt, my longing onto the page. The sketch took shape -- a heart, torn down the middle, one half dark and twisted, the other soft and glowing.

"That's it," Rabbit murmured, glancing at my drawing. "Let it flow out of you. There's no right or wrong in art."

I swallowed hard, my vision blurring with unshed tears. The pencil felt like an extension of my soul, giving voice to the war raging inside me.

"I don't know what to do, Rabbit," I whispered, my hand never stopping its frenzied dance across the paper. "I'm so confused. It's tearing me up."

Rabbit nodded, his own pencil still moving. "I know that feeling all too well. Like you're being ripped in two, yeah?"

I nodded, blinking back tears. The sketch pad was a mirror, reflecting my inner turmoil in stark black and white.

"Just keep drawing," Rabbit said. "Let the art do the talking. We'll figure this out together."

And so I did. I poured my heart onto the page, letting the pencil lead the way. The longer I drew, the calmer I felt.

I sneaked a glance at Rabbit's drawing -- a shadowy figure, hunched and alone, with a single beam of light breaking through the darkness.

"Art has been my therapy for years," he said, his eyes never leaving the page. "When the anxiety gets to be too much, when the club's problems weigh me down or nightmares from the past raise their heads, I draw. Once I'm finished, it's like I can breathe again."

I nodded, understanding all too well. The pressure in my chest eased with each stroke of the pencil, the knot in my stomach slowly unraveling.

"I've never been good at talking about my feelings," I admitted, shading in the jagged edges of the broken heart. "But this... this feels right."

Rabbit's lips quirked in a small smile. "That's the beauty of art, Eliza. It speaks when words fail us. It's a language all its own."

We lapsed into comfortable silence, the only sounds the scratching of pencils and our steady breathing. The kitchen faded away, and for a moment, it was just us and the art, lost in a world of our own making.

As I added the final touches to my sketch, I felt a sense of catharsis wash over me. The drawing was raw, painful, but it was also honest. It was a piece of my soul, laid bare on the page.

"Thank you, Rabbit," I whispered, my voice thick with emotion. "For this, for everything. I don't know what I would've done without you."

He reached across the table, his hand warm and reassuring on mine. "You're not alone. Never forget that."

And as I looked into his eyes, seeing the understanding and compassion shining there, I realized I'd found my place in this world, here with these tough men.

I took a deep breath, steeling myself for the words I was about to say. "It's just... I felt so confused, Rabbit. About Cheshire, about everything."

Rabbit set down his pencil, giving me his full attention. "What about Cheshire, Eliza?"

I bit my lip, the guilt twisting in my gut. "I know I shouldn't feel this way, not after what my father did. But when I'm with Cheshire, it's like nothing else matters. He makes me feel safe, understood. Desired." My cheeks warmed. "Then I think about the lives my father has destroyed, and I hate myself for being this happy."

Rabbit's eyes softened with empathy. "Eliza, listen to me. Your feelings for Cheshire... They aren't wrong. You can't help who you love. And after everything you've been through, you've more than earned the right to find happiness wherever and whenever you can. Your father's sins aren't your own."

"But how could I love him, Rabbit? How could I feel anything but disgust for myself, knowing what my father did to the people in this town?" My voice cracked, the tears threatening to spill over. "I may not have known about it, had no power to stop it, but I feel tainted because I share the same blood as that man."

Rabbit leaned forward, his gaze intense. "I'll say it once more. What your father did, that was on him. Not you. You weren't responsible for his actions, Eliza. You hear me? You need to let that shit go."

I nodded, a single tear escaping down my cheek.

"And as for Cheshire," Rabbit continued. "He's a good man. He cares about you, Eliza. Anyone with eyes can see that."

I sniffed, wiping away the tear with the back of my hand. "It's so hard, Rabbit. It feels like a betrayal to everyone else who's suffered at my father's hands."

Rabbit shook his head. "No one would ever think that, Eliza. I'm not sure what the plan is yet for handling the town. If we find those missing girls, and they come home, they may tell people your father was responsible. I don't know if Cheshire and Hatter are going to tell them the truth, that we handled the problem and the sheriff won't be an issue anymore, or if they're going to fabricate something."

"Thank you, Rabbit," I whispered. "For understanding, for not judging me. And for the advice. I've never felt so at home anywhere before. All of you feel more like family than my father ever did."

He smiled. "That's what family's for, Eliza. And yes, we're your family. We love you, no matter what. Never forget that."

I felt a weight lift from my shoulders. I didn't have all the answers, but I knew one thing for sure: with my Underland family by my side, I could face whatever came next, even if it meant battling my own demons.

Rabbit flipped through his sketch pad, revealing page after page of intricate drawings. Motorcycles, portraits, abstract designs. They were all really good. Good enough to hang in an art gallery.

I studied the sketches, marveling at the raw emotion captured in each line. "I didn't know you were so talented, Rabbit," I murmured, tracing a finger over a particularly haunting portrait. "These are beyond amazing."

He shrugged, a small smile tugging at his lips. "It's not about talent. It's about expression. About letting go of all the shit that weighs me down and just creating something. Anything. I never know what's going to end up on the page."

I nodded, understanding dawning. My gaze fell to my own sketch. "Art therapy."

"Exactly. And the best part? You can do it anytime, anywhere. Whenever you need to let it out, just pick up a pencil and let it flow. Doesn't matter if you're alone or with a group of people."

I flipped to a new page in the sketch pad he'd given me. As I put pencil to paper once more, I felt a sense of purpose, of direction. I might not be able to change the past, but I could face the future head-on. One sketch at a time.

Time slipped away as Rabbit and I lost ourselves in our artwork. The kitchen became a sanctuary, a place where we could bare our souls without fear of judgment or ridicule. Although, I knew no one here at the clubhouse would ever condemn me for my thoughts and feelings. Not unless I did something to hurt myself or the club.

I glanced up from my sketch, studying Rabbit's face as he worked. His brow was furrowed in concentration, his hand moving with a surety that came from years of practice. In that moment, he looked different. Lighter, somehow. The nervous energy that seemed to be such a big part of him melted away when he was drawing.

"I never knew how much I needed this," I confessed.

"I'm happy to draw with you anytime. I know Jo showed you her poems. Did you see her sketchbook? She's one hell of an artist. I know she'd be happy to draw with you any time."

"Thank you, Rabbit," I said, my voice thick with emotion. "For this. For everything."

He reached across the table, giving my hand a gentle squeeze. "Anytime, Eliza."

And in that moment, I realized Rabbit was my friend. A true friend, who saw me for who I was and accepted me, flaws and all. I'd not had a friend, ever. I'd never realized what it would feel like to be close to someone like this, to be accepted. Now I had many. Jo, Rabbit, and everyone else here. Except Cheshire... he was something more.

"Probably should wrap it up for now," Rabbit said. "Jo will be in here any minute to start dinner. I bet she'd love some company."

I nodded. "I can help too. I'm not the best cook, but I can at least do something, even if it's chopping vegetables."

We packed up the supplies, and Rabbit held out his hand. "I'll take it to your room and leave it on the bed."

I handed it off to him and waited for Jo. It didn't take her long to enter the kitchen, a smile on her face.

"I saw Rabbit. He said you're my helper tonight?"

"Yeah. But I told him I'm not a very good cook." I wasn't sure if I'd be a help or a hindrance.

"That's okay. I'm not the best either. I'm learning as I go." She placed a hand over her belly. "Need to figure all this out before the little one gets here."

My eyes went wide. "You're pregnant?"

She nodded. "Yep. Hatter hasn't told everyone yet, though, so keep it quiet. Only Rabbit and Cheshire know."

I made the motion of locking my lips. "I won't say anything."

"I trust you, Eliza. Now, come help. We're making chicken wraps with onion and bell pepper."

"Sounds yummy." I moved closer to her. "What do you need me to do?"

"Well, you can start by setting the table. Then you can get the tortillas from the cabinet and warm them."

"Um, how do I warm them?" I asked.

"Grab a skillet, set the heat to low, then place one on it. Let it sit for thirty to sixty seconds, flip it for another thirty seconds, then move on to the next one. It shouldn't stick. If it does, then you're leaving them on too long. They won't still be hot when the boys come in to eat, but they'll still be tasty."

I did as Jo said, and as I warmed the tortillas, I watched her slice chicken breasts into small strips. She pulled out one bottle of seasoning, and I kept waiting for her to grab more. Didn't recipes usually call for several?

She eyed me. "I haven't told the guys, but I only use seasonings that either have no sodium or are low in sodium. I even have a salt substitute. This particular blend is just warm enough to have a good flavor without being too hot."

Once she had the chicken cooking, she alternated between stirring the chicken around the skillet and slicing bell pepper and onion. I wondered why she was doing it that way, when I realized she still had chicken strips to cook. She shifted the cooked ones into a serving bowl, then started cooking the next batch.

Jo pulled out a covered skillet and put a little oil in it, then turned on the burner. Once I heard the oil sizzling, she dropped in the peppers and onions, stirring them at regular intervals. The second batch of chicken went into the serving bowl, and she turned down the heat on the peppers and onions before covering them.

"One last batch of chicken and then we can eat," she said. "Want to go tell everyone? Looks like you've finished the tortillas. You can place the plate on the table."

I set them in the center of the table and went into the main room, then drew in a breath and yelled as loud as I could, "Dinner is almost done!"

March chuckled from where he'd been sitting a few feet away, but I heard booted steps coming down the hall. At least it seemed they might have all heard me. I went back to help Jo finish up, and once we sat down to eat and I had my first bite, I stared at Jo in awe. The meal was simple, yet so incredibly good.

"Sometimes I make cilantro lime rice and black beans to go with it," Jo said. "But not always. There are times simpler is better."

"You did good," Hatter said. "They came out perfect."

Jo winked at me. "Eliza warmed the tortillas for me and set the table."

"Maybe I can help more next time, since I know what to do now."

Jo nodded. "Sounds good. I should have done the prep earlier, but…"

If she'd tried to come to the kitchen earlier, she would have seen me drawing with Rabbit. I had a feeling that instead of letting us know she was there, she would have backed off and given us space.

Meals with the club really did feel like a family affair. I wondered what the holidays would be like.

Chapter Thirteen

Cheshire

After dinner, everyone tended to scatter to their rooms or linger in the common area. Since Eliza had been alone for so long, I was taking a gamble on her not wanting to feel isolated right now. If I didn't see her, then I'd know she was in her room, and I'd give her space. But I was eager to spend time with her. She'd already gotten under my skin. All it took was a smile from her, and I would do anything she asked of me.

The dim light in the far corner of the Underland MC clubhouse cast long shadows across the leather couch. I'd found Eliza in this quiet corner.

"Cheshire," she whispered.

I took a step, my boots thudding against the floor. The world narrowed to just us, the noise fading into nothing. Her gaze held me captive, a siren's call I couldn't resist. My heart had been pounding out a rhythm that screamed her name.

"Eliza," I said. Just saying her name made me happy.

She had been close enough that I could see the rise and fall of her chest, quick and uneven. I reached out, slowly, deliberately. My fingertips grazed her cheek, brushing a rebellious strand of hair behind her ear.

"Cheshire," she murmured again, briefly closing her eyes and leaning into my touch.

"Shhh." My hand lingered on her face, my thumb stroking her skin. Couldn't help it. Every time I looked into her eyes, I felt so lost. Powerless.

I breathed her in, and I could smell the soap she used to wash up. If it were quiet in here, I wondered if

I'd be able to hear her heartbeat. I wanted her, more than I'd ever wanted anything.

"Eliza, I won't deny what I feel for you. I want you. I think you feel the same, but... I'm worried I'll move too fast. I don't want to overwhelm you."

"Cheshire." She paused. "No... Charlie. When I'm with you, I feel like I'm on fire. My heart races, and it feels like something is buzzing under my skin. Anticipation, or maybe... I don't know. I don't have a label for it."

Damn if her words didn't hit me like a freight train. I'd already told her she was mine, but hearing the words made it all seem new. It amazed me I could make her feel that way. From the first moment I'd taken her to my room, I'd worried I was merely someone to sate her curiosity. Even after unofficially claiming her, some part of me had wondered if she really understood and accepted what it meant. She was so damn innocent, but now I wondered if I could hope for something real, a passion that could burn brighter than all the stars in the sky.

"Eliza." I wanted to tell her everything, lay it all out bare. But words didn't come easily. So I showed her.

I tugged her against my body, tipping her chin up. As badly as I wanted to kiss her, I wasn't sure she'd want that in front of everyone. Instead, I let her see the desire I knew had to be burning in my gaze.

"Tell me," I rasped. "Tell me you're mine."

"Cheshire. I want to be with you. If you want to call me yours, then I think I'd like that. A lot."

"God, Eliza..." My lips twisted into a half-smile as I fought the beast of desire gnawing at my restraint. I wanted her. Here. Now. But my sweet little innocent Eliza deserved better. I whispered her name again, my breath ghosting her lips. It was a tease, a taste of sin I wasn't sure we should indulge in. But damn me, I wanted it.

Her scent wrapped around me, all sweet and floral, out of place in the grit and shadows of the clubhouse. My chest was tight, wound up with a mix of need and something else -- something that felt too much like... love. But it was far too soon for the L word.

She leaned against me even more. Staring up into my eyes, she parted her lips, as if begging for a kiss. Then she damned us both by uttering the words.

"Kiss me," she said. It shredded the last of my control. I was the club's Vice President. I was supposed to be all cool calculation and strategy. But none of that mattered right now, not with her voice threading through my thoughts like a siren's song.

I captured her mouth, gave in to the heat. It was a searing connection that branded me, scorched away the shadows. Her lips were soft, warm, and all the warnings in my head turned to dust.

I didn't care who might be watching. Didn't care that we weren't in the privacy of my room. I needed to taste her. To own her in whatever way possible.

"Eliza," I muttered against her mouth, tasting her sweetness. Her hands, tentative at first, found the edges of my cut, pulling me closer. And I was lost in her.

Heat. It was all I felt, all I was. Eliza's lips under mine, her breath mingling with my own. I was teetering on a cliff.

"Charlie," she whispered, and that's when I snapped.

I jerked back, gasping for air like I'd been underwater too long. My heart hammered against my ribcage, every beat screaming at me to take her, claim her. But I couldn't. Wouldn't. Not like this.

"I can't lose control, Eliza. Not with you." The words came out hard, edged with desperation.

She blinked up at me, confusion clouding those big eyes. They were wide, too damn innocent. I saw longing there, a mirror of my own. With anyone else, I might have tossed them over my shoulder and carried them off to bed. But not with her.

"I need to protect you," I said, forcing the words out even as my body screamed to close the distance between us again. "And that means keeping a distance until we're out of danger. I can't risk screwing things up because you're on my mind even more than you already are."

"Distance?" she asked. She watched me, her face unreadable. "Out of danger."

Her brow furrowed, and my fingers itched to reach up and smooth the worry lines. But I'd caused them and didn't have the right to reach for her. Not now.

Her hand shot out, fingers clutching the edge of my cut. I stared at her fingers, where they gripped the leather.

"Eliza." My tone held a note of warning. I was so close to losing it.

"Worried?" Her eyes were wide, searching mine -- seeking truth or lies, I couldn't tell.

"Yes," I admitted. She held my gaze, and I knew I was losing the battle. "Damnit. Listen, Eliza. This isn't a good idea."

No matter what I said, she didn't release me. If anything, she seemed to hold on even tighter. A part of me was glad, because I honestly didn't want her to let me go.

Before I realized what she was doing, Eliza closed the gap between us, pressing her lips to mine. "What if I don't want to wait? What if waiting means we can never be together?"

I had always known she was brave. Bold. But this? This was something else. I'd never thought she'd be the one to initiate a kiss, much less ask for more.

"Eliza..." My throat tightened. I couldn't breathe. I couldn't think.

She was right. Every damn word.

Holmes. That bastard. If things went south, this could be my final mission, the one that put an end to me. She was looking at me, eyes blazing. Daring me to choose. Live for now or die waiting. I'd never been one to back down from a challenge, and I wasn't going to start now.

"Fuck." My voice was nearly a growl, low, torn from deep within. "Lead the way."

She smiled with a fearless spark in her gaze. Eliza took my hand and pulled me through the hallways of the clubhouse. The thump of bass from the bar area faded behind us.

"Your room," she whispered, a devilish promise.

I let her lead, relinquishing control. We reached the door. My sanctuary. Our escape.

"Inside." My command was ragged, desperate. Maybe I wasn't as good at giving up control as I'd thought.

The lock clicked behind us, sealing away the world. Just Eliza and me. Nothing else mattered.

I gripped her waist, pulling Eliza to me with a force that left no question about my need. Her body was soft against mine, fitting like she's been made for this, for me.

"Cheshire..." Her voice was a breathy whisper,

but I didn't let her finish.

"Shh." I silenced her with a kiss that stole our breaths, rough and all-consuming. It was like an out-of-control wildfire, the kind of kiss that branded your soul. I was lost in the taste of her, the feel of her.

Clothes became trivial barriers. I fumbled with the hem of her shirt, desperate to feel her skin against mine. Then -- a knock. Sharp, insistent. Reality came crashing back.

"Damn it." I closed my eyes, trying to reel in my emotions.

Eliza's eyes mirrored my frustration, her chest heaving against mine. Our moment, teetering on the edge of being lost, was now gone. We were silent, listening as footsteps retreated from the door.

"Cheshire?" Her voice was questioning, her gaze searching my face for what came next.

I leaned in and pressed my forehead to hers. Close enough to share breath, to feel her every exhale. "I don't know, doll," I admitted. "I get the feeling it's important and I need to go see what they need. But you and me? If we can ever just… be… then we'll pick up where we left off."

I kissed her once more and left the room. Why did it feel like fate was trying to kick me in the balls? As much as I wanted Eliza, she always seemed to be just slightly out of reach. Maybe I shouldn't have let her go the last time I had her in my bed.

* * *

Eliza

I watched Cheshire walk away, leaving me alone with my heart fluttering and my hands shaking. I sank onto his bed, his scent drifting up from his blankets. I felt entirely too aware of him. Pressing a hand to my mouth, I wished I could hold onto the sensation of him kissing me. Worry ate at me. What if he went after my father and didn't come back? What if we missed our chance of being together?

I heard footsteps outside the door and glanced up, hoping it was Cheshire. Instead, Jo stood in the doorway. She gave me a sad smile and sighed.

"Looks like my night wasn't the only one ruined. March had an idea of how to handle things with your father and the others. Think the club is meeting to discuss it."

"Then I guess the night is over…" I flopped back on Cheshire's bed. "I'm starting to think I'm going to die a virgin."

Jo snorted and laughed. "I don't think that's going to happen. As swollen as your lips are, Cheshire definitely wants you. The timing is just off."

"How do you do it?" I asked, glancing her way again. "The waiting and not knowing, the interruptions…"

Jo shrugged a shoulder. "What the club is doing is important. Not only for your safety, but for this town as well. I just try to keep that in mind. I'm not saying I don't get frustrated. I do. Doesn't change the fact the Underland MC is fighting a battle they need to win if this town has a chance of surviving."

I nodded, understanding what she was saying. I knew it, deep down, but it didn't change the fact it felt like Cheshire was constantly being snatched away from me.

"It sucks, but hang in there," Jo said. "I promise things will get better. Once they take down your father, the mayor, and his righthand man, Robert Lewis, things will improve around here."

"You mean until another disaster strikes?" I

asked.

"Maybe. Hard to say what will happen in the future. The question is whether you're ready to stay by his side and fight alongside him or give up and move on with your life elsewhere. Because if you stay in Warren, Cheshire will never let you go. I've seen the way he watches you. The man may as well have already tattooed his name on you."

I pressed a hand to my chest. "I think he did, right here over my heart."

Jo threw her head back and laughed. "Don't tell him that. He may actually put his name there. Out of all of them, I think Cheshire is probably the craziest."

"I'm scared, Jo." I sat up and joined her at the doorway. We left Cheshire's room and stood in the hallway. "I'm terrified something will happen to him. I've never been so happy before. What if this is all a dream and I wake up back in hell?"

Jo reached for my hand, giving it a squeeze. "You won't. It's reality, Eliza. Just hold on to him with all you've got… and ride out the storm as best you can."

Jo walked me to my room, and I lay awake for hours. Closing my eyes, I'd done my best to envision my future with Cheshire. Did he want a family? Would we always live here at the clubhouse? Would our lives always be filled with danger and chaos?

At some point, I fell into a restless sleep, my dreams plagued by nightmares. Cheshire dying at my father's hands, in multiple ways. Over and over… but the worst part was how helpless I felt each time, unable to stop it from happening. I had no choice but to cry over his lifeless body, unable to change what happened, even when I knew it was coming.

By the time I woke in the morning, my head ached and my heart hurt. What would I do if those dreams became a reality? I didn't think I could handle losing him. Wasn't sure I wanted to.

With my thoughts dark and heavy, I forced myself out of bed. Whether I wanted to or not, I needed to get up and face the day head-on.

Chapter Fourteen

Cheshire

The first rays of dawn sliced through the blinds. I rolled onto my back, the sheets tangling around my legs -- a poor man's embrace compared to Eliza's touch. Would she be in bed with me right now if we hadn't been interrupted? Or would I have found the strength to hold back once more?

I slung my arm over my eyes, blocking out the light but not the images of Eliza playing in my mind. Flashes of her smile, the curve of her hip, the innocent look in her eyes -- they played on repeat, a damn film reel I couldn't shut off.

Frustration built inside me. Her image was burned into my mind, seared onto every damn thought. It was more than wanting. It was a hunger, clawing from the inside out. Even now, my cock was hard as a fucking rock.

I shoved my hand down inside my boxers and started stroking. The mere thought of her lying under me, legs splayed, my name on her lips, was nearly enough to make me come. I pumped my cock in quick, short strokes, biting back a groan as I came all over my hand. I hadn't been that quick since high school.

I threw the covers off, my skin prickling. The air was cool, but it didn't touch the burn under my skin. Each breath was heavier, thick with desire for her, and I knew -- I was done fighting this. But first I needed to clean myself up.

Eliza. Her name was a bullet, shot straight through the armor I'd built. She was the wrench in my plans, the unexpected twist in my road -- my road that had always been clear and straight.

I ran a hand through my hair. The club, my

brothers, relied on me to be sharp, to think ahead. But now, it was like I was wading through mud, her pull dragging me down, deeper and darker.

"Damn woman," I whispered, half-curse and half-plea. There was no choice left. I had to have her, had to claim what was mine.

I went into the bathroom and ran the shower. After I stripped off my boxers, I tossed them into the hamper in the corner and stepped under the spray. A quick scrub was enough to clean away the evidence of what I'd done and clear the cobwebs in my brain. More awake and alert, I was ready to find the woman haunting me day and night.

I threw on a clean pair of boxers and tugged on a T-shirt. Hatter would probably lose his shit if he saw me leave my room like this. I had a feeling he and Jo were still asleep. I was counting on it. If not, I'd get my ass handed to me.

The floor was cold as hell under my bare feet. I stalked toward the door, yanking it open with a force that made the hinges protest. Now that I'd decided what I would do, there was no point waiting.

Eliza was under my skin, a fever I couldn't sweat out.

I stepped into the hallway, the dim light throwing shadows across the walls. They were like ghosts, whispering her name, echoing the throb in my veins. The clubhouse was quiet, most of the brothers still knocked out or passed out, resting up for whatever chaos we were diving into next.

But there was no rest for the wicked, and right now a devil was sitting on my shoulder, whispering Eliza's name, urging me to snatch her and run.

She was the itch I had to scratch, the storm I had to chase. The tension coiled tighter inside me with each step. Every sound was too loud in my ears -- the soft snoring from one of the rooms, the rustle of sheets as someone turned over in their sleep.

But none of that mattered. It was all background noise. Static.

Where was she? Still in her room? I made my way to the common area, just in case she'd had a sleepless night. If she wanted me anywhere near as much as I wanted her, then she wouldn't have been able to sleep well.

The common area was dim, with only a few slivers of light cutting through the blinds. And then I saw her. Eliza. She sat on the worn-out couch like she was part of the shadows herself.

Her gaze lifted, catching mine. "Cheshire," she whispered.

I didn't say anything. I didn't need to. One step after another, I drew closer to her. Eliza watched me, her breath hitching just enough that I noticed. Good. It meant she was every bit as affected by me as I was by her.

I was close now, could almost feel the heat coming off her skin. I reached out, my hand wrapping around hers. It was a lifeline, pulling her into my world, into the chaos that had been building inside me since the second I laid eyes on her.

I helped her off the couch without a word and started leading her to my room. I could tell she was trying to keep up, her slight frame swaying slightly.

The hallway stretched out, seeming endless. Anticipation coiled tight in my gut with each step. It was a hunger, gnawing at me, desperate to be sated.

"Where are we --" she started, but I cut her off with a look.

"Shh," I said, finger pressed against her lips,

silencing the question she didn't need answered. She nodded, understanding the unspoken promise hanging heavy between us. The door loomed ahead, and I knew what waited on the other side -- heat, desire, release. It was a collision course we'd been on since the moment our eyes locked. And I was ready for the impact.

The door clicked shut, the sound echoing like a final note to a prelude. My hand rested on the knob for a second longer than necessary, a barrier between us and the rest of the club. The world outside ceased to exist. It was just me and Eliza, enclosed in the sanctity of dim shadows. I twisted the lock just to make sure we wouldn't be interrupted.

The room's low light wrapped around us, turning everything velvety and soft. It felt like we were standing at the center of a storm, electricity crackling in the silence between us.

Her wide, innocent eyes anchored me. Shadows played across her face, but they couldn't hide the flush I knew was there.

Her presence in my sanctuary was a fire that warmed the chill of my bones, chased away the edge that always lingered in my gut. Here, in this room, the world's noise was muffled, replaced by the thrumming in my veins, the rush in my ears. Every breath I took was heavy with her scent, sweet and spicy.

We stood there, two lost souls drawn together, a magnetic pull too strong to resist. I saw it in her gaze -- the same wildfire that was burning through my restraint. I didn't feel words were needed. Not now. Her lips parted, as if begging to be kissed.

I stepped in, closing the gap. I placed my hands, rough from years of wrenching on bikes and throwing punches, on the curve of her waist. They fit there like they were molded for this very purpose -- to pull her into me, to claim the space between us as ours alone.

The distance was gone. Her body's heat seeped into mine, set my blood on fire. The room's shadows wrapped around us like a shroud, and in this dim light, we were all that existed. The rest of the world could burn, and I wouldn't give a damn. She was here with me, and I was about to cross a line I couldn't come back from. Not that I wanted to.

Her lips crashed against mine, fierce and demanding. The world narrowed down to the pressure of her mouth. I reached up to tangle my hand in her hair, pulling her closer, kissing her deeper. Eliza's fingers clawed at my back, desperate, as if she wanted to pull me into her very soul.

"Cheshire," she gasped between kisses, her voice ragged and desperate. I tasted the need on her tongue, a hunger to match my own. Every kiss was a battle, every touch a claim staked.

We stripped out of our clothes with reckless abandon. Her shirt hit the floor, then mine, the chill of the air nothing against the heat we generated. I watched hungrily as she unfastened her bra and let it drop. I bit my lip to keep myself from leaning in and tasting her pretty nipples. As she shimmied out of her jeans, dragging her panties down too, I had to fight back a groan. My cock was so fucking hard right now! I made quick work ditching boxers, not wanting so much as a thread between us. I needed to feel her skin against mine.

"God, Cheshire," she whimpered, and it was like throwing gasoline on the blaze. I couldn't think of anything sweeter than the way she said my name.

Skin against skin, we collided -- a dance as old as time, frenzied and fervent. There was no room for thought, only instinct. I tried to tell myself to slow down, to take it easy. I knew it was her first time, and yet, I no longer had control over myself.

"Mine," I said, my voice ringing with the possession I felt to my very bones. She answered with a moan, her nails digging into my shoulders, branding me as surely as any ink that had ever touched my skin.

"I need you," she murmured.

"You know what I want. What I need." I kissed her again, my lips devouring hers. "And I'm going to take it. So, if this is too much, if you've changed your mind, now is the time to tell me."

She shook her head. "I'm yours. I always was."

Our bodies were pressed tightly together, and I took a small step back so I could look at her beauty. Reaching out, I lightly ran my fingers between her breasts, watching as her nipples puckered. In that moment, I knew what she needed. Someone to take charge, someone who would make her feel safe, yet desired.

I claimed her lips in a passionate kiss that left us both panting. Pressing her against the door, I slid my hand up her thigh. As I nipped at her bottom lip, I trailed my fingers over her sensitive skin, teasing her.

She arched her back, pushing herself farther into my touch. "You like that, don't you?"

Tracing the lips of her wet pussy, I groaned at the scent of her arousal and delved deeper, rubbing her clit in small circles. Her hips bucked against my hand, and she gasped out my name.

"You're so fucking tight," I whispered against her ear, licking the lobe, as I eased a finger inside her.

She whimpered, unable to resist any longer. "Charlie, please!"

I withdrew my hand, leaving her aching with anticipation. Then, without warning, I lifted her up and carried her to the bed. Her legs splayed and I settled between them. Eliza shuddered as I lapped at her sweet nectar like a starving man. My tongue explored every inch of her. I teased her swollen clit, and I pushed my tongue inside her.

She cried out, her fingers tangling in my hair. "Oh, God, right there!"

I flicked her clit with my tongue, watching as she buckled under the intense pleasure. I thrust my finger into her again, using slow, shallow thrusts. Her pussy clenched as she came undone. My cock throbbed, aching to be inside her.

"Turn over," I commanded, my voice rough with desire. I knew I should be gentle. Should take her facing me, but I needed to see if she could handle all of me.

She obeyed without question, presenting her ass to me. I smacked her plump cheeks, leaving a red imprint of my hand. She yelped and gripped the sheets, but I saw a flush on her face that told me she'd enjoyed it.

"Such a good girl," I murmured, positioning myself at her entrance. She trembled as I entered her slowly, feeling every inch of my thickness stretching her tight pussy. I bit back a groan at how incredible she felt. "Am I hurting you?"

She shook her head and buried her face in the bedding. I started slowly, giving her time to adjust. Even if I wanted to see if she could take me, I also didn't want to cause her pain. The next time she clenched, I knew I couldn't hold back.

I slammed into her, claiming her body as my own with frantic thrusts. Her cries of pleasure only fueled my passion, and I slid in and out of her pussy with long, deep strokes. She begged for more as we lost ourselves in the heat of the moment.

I felt my release building inside me. Refusing to come before she did, I eased my hand between her legs and played with her clit. The moment she came, calling out my name, I grabbed her hips tightly and pounded into her. It only took a few strokes before I filled her up with my cum.

And that's when I realized how badly I'd just fucked up. *Shit!*

"Fucking hell," I muttered. "Eliza, I'm so damn sorry."

She blinked at me as she rolled to her side. "It didn't hurt. I mean, I'm sore, but..."

I shook my head. "Not that. I didn't use a condom. I stopped before because I didn't have one, but just now... I didn't even think about it. I was going to stop by the store and grab some, but something came up and I never made it."

She stared at me, her eyes wide. With a shaky hand, she reached for her belly, pressing her palm against it. Yeah. I could have very well knocked her up without meaning to. And I'd already told her if that happened, I'd never let her go. Fucking hell. If she thought about that, it would probably freak her out.

"I'm an idiot. I never would have..." I closed my eyes and pinched the bridge of my nose. Too late now. "Look, I'm only saying this because it should have been your choice. After everything you've been through, the last thing I'd want to do is force a pregnancy on you. I seem to lose my head around you."

"But you aren't sorry because you regret being with me?" she asked.

"What? Fuck no!" I stretched out beside her, pulling her into my arms. "Eliza, I could never regret claiming you as my own. But we haven't talked about kids, or what our future might look like. I may have just robbed you of the chance to decide all that for yourself. When I told you before that a baby would change things, I meant it."

She cupped my cheek. "The fact you're worried about it is enough. We can always use protection next time. If it turns out later that I'm pregnant, then maybe it was meant to happen. As for me being yours... I thought we already decided I was."

I wanted to argue the point, but I couldn't. If we didn't have a tie like a kid, then I'd never make her stay if she was miserable. Hell, even with a kid, I wasn't sure I could do that to her. Her happiness meant everything to me, especially after all she'd been through. Then her words really hit me...

"Are you saying you don't believe in coincidences? That your father was destined to beat the hell out of you? Because you can't justify this and not that." The mere thought of it infuriated me.

"If he hadn't, I wouldn't have run away. And if I hadn't run, then I wouldn't have met you. So yeah, I think everything happens for a reason."

I couldn't understand her. If we were supposed to be together, then I had to believe fate would have found a way... without her having to endure so much pain all her life.

"I'm yours now, right?" Eliza asked.

"Yeah, doll. You're mine." I kissed her temple. "Not ever letting you go."

"Good." She snuggled against me.

"If someone had asked me if I'd ever get caught by a woman, fall for her and want to keep her by my side, I'd have said no fucking way. But you caught me, Eliza. From the moment I first saw you, I was yours."

"You caught me too," she whispered back, and those simple words slammed into me harder than any fist ever could.

"Love you." The confession took me by surprise. Even though I may have thought the words, I hadn't intended to say them. I glanced at her, wondering if she'd heard me.

Her eyes glowed in the dim light.

"Charlie…" I could hear the wonderment in her voice, a softness I had never known I wanted until now.

"Every damn inch, Eliza. Love every damn inch of you."

"I love you too," she said, as she reached for me. She pressed her hand to my cheek. For a guy who was always a step ahead, this moment was uncharted territory -- a place where the cunning Cheshire faded into the background, and Charlie Collins, the man who'd found something worth holding onto, had emerged. Until now, I hadn't realized there were two sides of me.

This woman was more than I deserved, but I'd be damned if I'd let anyone take her from me.

Chapter Fifteen
Cheshire

My phone's ring broke the silence in the garage. I'd stepped out here to clear my head, and thankfully the place was empty. I snatched up the phone, the screen flashing "Unknown Caller." My gut clenched. Nothing good ever came from calls like these.

"Talk to me," I said as I accepted the call, then pressed the speaker button.

"Cheshire," the voice sounded distorted, like it had been scrambled electronically. "Sheriff knows you've got Eliza. He's coming for her."

The line went dead. I stared at the phone, my jaw tightening until it ached. Sheriff Holmes, that twisted son of a bitch, breathing down our necks again. And Eliza -- Goddamn it, she wasn't going back to that hellhole.

"Cheshire, what's wrong?" Knave's voice pulled me back, his eyes narrowing at the look on my face. I hadn't even heard him come out here.

"Sheriff's on the move," I said, my voice low and steady, even though I felt anything but. "He wants Eliza."

Knave's fists clenched, veins popping on his tattooed arms. "Not happening."

"Damn straight." I slid my phone into my pocket and turned on my heel, heading for where my bike stood, gleaming under the flickering lights. "We hit him first. That's the only way to keep her safe."

"Are we ready?" Mock asked, skepticism in his tone as he joined us.

"Doesn't matter. We've got no choice." Rabbit and Carpenter came into the garage as well, probably sensing something was about to happen. "Rabbit, care to join us?"

"I'm there if you need me," he said, the fire in his eyes telling me he was all in. For once, his anxiety seemed almost nonexistent.

We had to keep Eliza safe, had to take down Sheriff Holmes before he could lay another finger on her, or anyone else. The club was my family, but Eliza... she was something more, something worth fighting for. We weren't just defending her. We were declaring war. It had been a fight that started when Jo showed up, and I knew it wouldn't end until we'd taken them all down. But the shit with Jo had been more of a skirmish. Well, several of them until we'd finally ended Eddie Lewis. This was different. Even though Eddie had been connected to some pretty powerful people, it was nothing compared to taking on the sheriff and mayor's office.

I knew one thing for certain: this was it. No turning back. We were heading straight into the storm, and hell itself couldn't stop us now. I'd do whatever it took to make that man pay for all his sins.

I stopped not too far from the clubhouse when I saw a familiar vehicle outside the diner. I pulled over and went inside, finding Park in one of the booths. The moment he saw me, the fury coming off me in waves, he understood what was happening.

"Where's he holed up?" Fuck pleasantries. I didn't have time for it.

"Warehouse on the edge of town," Park said, tapping his phone screen, sending the location to mine. "Got a nasty nest of vipers with him. I'd debated telling you."

"Well, I got an anonymous call telling me the sheriff is after Eliza. It's not like I'm going to sit back and let it happen."

Park's jaw tightened and he gave a sharp nod. "Right. If she's in trouble, then you have to go."

I still didn't like the way he talked about her, but for now he was on our side, and I needed all the allies I could get. I went back out to my bike and led my brothers to the warehouse's location. It loomed ahead, ugly and rusting, and surrounded by goons who looked like trouble had birthed them. Too many.

"Looks like a full house," I muttered, eyeing the rough crew through narrowed lids.

"Party crashers, that's us," Mock said with a twisted smile that didn't reach his eyes. He knew as well as I did this could get bloody.

"Stay sharp," I warned, cutting the engine, the silence sudden and heavy. We were four against a horde, but we had steel wills and iron fists. We didn't have a choice if we wanted to survive.

"Always am," Rabbit said, though his hand trembled as he checked to see what weapons he had on him. With Rabbit, there was always a chance he'd hidden things in his clothes or boots without realizing it. I'd watched him on several occasions, and it was like his hands and brain weren't always connected. He'd often pull something from his pocket and stare at it like he had no clue how it had gotten there.

"Let's make some noise," Knave said, and it wasn't excitement in his voice but the calm before a storm.

Leaving wasn't an option now. The men spotted us and started to move. "Take them down!" I yelled, as I charged.

Knave was a shadow on my right, his fists hammers against pounding flesh and bone. Mock's wild laughter cut through the din, a manic soundtrack to the chaos he sowed with every swing. Rabbit, quick and wiry, ducked and dodged like he'd been born in a brawl.

Thankfully, none of the sheriff's men had pulled a weapon yet. Part of me wondered why and found it odd, but if it meant we had a chance at a fair fight, I'd take it.

"Cheshire!" Knave's voice, a warning. I twisted just in time, avoiding an uppercut to my jaw.

We moved as one, but these bastards were tough -- tougher than we'd anticipated. They absorbed our hits, retaliated with brutal precision. It wasn't just their strength. There was technique behind those punches. These weren't common thugs.

"Trained..." I grunted, blocking a kick aimed for my head. "These guys... are trained."

"Didn't sign up for easy," Mock shouted back, swinging wide and taking out two goons with a single blow.

"Keep at it!" The words ripped from my throat as I slammed my fist into another face. Couldn't think about the pain, the way my knuckles split and bled. Had to focus. Had to keep moving.

"Cheshire!"

I spun, Rabbit's call snapping me to attention. A monstrous brute bore down on him, muscles coiled and ready to strike. Without thinking, I intercepted, tackling the giant at the knees. We hit the ground, a tangle of limbs and fury.

"Thanks." Rabbit's nod was short, his eyes already scanning for the next threat.

"Anytime," I panted, rolling off the fallen enemy.

"Where's the sheriff?" Knave's voice cut through the noise, low and urgent.

"Back!" I pointed with a bloodied hand toward the figure watching us, his hands folded calmly behind his back. Sheriff Holmes. Always in control, even when his world was crashing down. Or maybe ours was the one being wrecked right now. It was hard to say who was winning.

"Go!" I pushed Knave toward him, even as I squared off against another attacker. "I got this!"

"Watch your six, Cheshire!" Mock called out before darting after Knave.

"Always do!" I smirked, despite the ache in my ribs, the fire in my blood. This was what we did, what we lived for. And for Eliza, who deserved a life free of the sheriff's grasp.

The battle raged on, seeming as if it would never end.

Blood dripped from my knuckles, the taste of iron hot on my tongue. I glared at the man before me -- just another obstacle between me and the sheriff. His eyes were dead set on mine, a mirror of my own resolve. We'd been trading blows for what felt like hours, each hit a promise to keep going until only one of us was left standing.

He lunged at me, a gleam of steel catching the light. Knife. I cursed under my breath and whipped out my blade, the curved, serrated edge perfect for doing some damage. Our dance turned deadly. He was good, slicing air inches from my face, but I was better -- or at least I had more to fight for.

His blade bit into my arm, a line of fire searing through flesh. Pain screamed up my limb, but it was just noise -- background static to the adrenaline pumping through my veins. I couldn't afford to falter, not now. Eliza's face flashed in my mind, her smile reminding me what I was fighting for.

"Is that all you've got?" I taunted, spinning away from another strike. My voice was ragged, edged with the strain of combat.

The man sneered, circling like a shark scenting blood. He didn't understand that every brother by my side was a reason to endure, to push past the burn in my muscles and the haze clouding my vision. That I had a sweet woman at home counting on me to put an end to this nightmare.

I parried his next attack, metal singing against metal. He was relentless, but so was I. They thought they could wear us down, take back what they believed was theirs. They didn't know the Underland MC -- the family I'd bleed for, the love I'd die for.

"Come on, you son of a bitch," I snarled.

"Cheshire!" Mock's shout pierced the chaos, but I couldn't look away, not even for a second. The battle was here, now.

My attacker pushed forward, trying to overpower me. But I stood firm.

"You'll never take her. I'll die before I let any of you lay a hand on her."

The air was thick with violence. My boots slid on the grit and blood of the parking lot. I'd cut the bastard far more times than he'd gotten me, and yet he was still standing, still coming at me like a charging bull.

"Cheshire!" Knave's voice cut through the noise, his fist connecting with some thug's jaw in a spray of spit and blood.

"Got this!" I yelled back, ducking a wild swing meant to lay me out cold. We were outnumbered but not outmatched.

I spun, a roundhouse kick sending another one of the sheriff's goons sprawling. He hit the pavement with a grunt, scrambling to rise. Rabbit was beside me then, a flash of silver in his hand as he took down a brute twice his size. Mock fought like a demon, a wicked laugh bursting from him each time he landed a blow.

"Watch it," I grunted as Rabbit ducked a pipe swung at his head. These fuckers had decided to bring the heat, and they were tiring us out. Probably the plan from the start.

"Thanks, brother," he spat, kicking the attacker's knees out from under him.

The fight was a blur -- a mess of adrenaline and instinct. I didn't think. I moved. Fought. Survived. Every strike I delivered was for Eliza, every block for my brothers.

Pain was just a whisper in the back of my mind, something to be acknowledged, then ignored. My sliced arm screamed with each movement, but it couldn't drown out the roar of battle. I hadn't survived IEDs, surprise attacks by insurgents, and all manner of other things while I'd been active duty just to lose to some damn local thugs now.

"End this shit!" I shouted, eyes scanning for Sheriff Holmes, but the fucker was nowhere in sight, his goons bearing the brunt of his cowardice.

"Finish them!" Knave roared back, his knuckles red and split.

It was down to the last few now, the ones still stupid or brave enough to stand. They swayed on their feet, battered and bloody. But the assholes just wouldn't stay down!

I locked eyes with the last man standing once Knave and Rabbit took down two more. A behemoth who clearly hadn't had enough. He charged, all rage and no finesse. I sidestepped, letting his momentum do half the work. Then, with a twist of my body and a surge of everything I had left, I drove my fist into his kidney.

He howled and staggered. A second punch to the throat silenced him, dropping him like a sack of dirt to the ground.

"Stay down," I snarled, standing over him, chest heaving, my grin fierce and feral.

His eyes rolled back, and he slumped unconscious. Around me, the sounds of conflict died away, replaced by heavy breaths and the distant wail of sirens. Son of a bitch! The bastard, Sheriff Holmes, had apparently called in the cavalry.

"Cheshire..." Mock's voice was somewhere between impressed and concerned.

"Let them come," I said, turning to face my brothers, my family. "We have more important things to handle. The sheriff is gone."

"Son of a bitch," Knave spat. "Knew he wouldn't have the guts to face us."

"Doesn't matter." I clenched my fists, feeling the sting of fresh cuts. "He'll keep coming for her. We need to be ready."

"Always are," Mock said, his voice steady despite the blood streaking down his face. "What's next, VP?"

"War," I said simply. "We protect Eliza. We crush anyone who tries to take her. End of story. And when all this is over with, we'll have carved the corruption out of Warren, and this town can begin to heal."

The sirens grew louder, closing in. We didn't need to be caught here. Not like this. If the sheriff called those men, then they were likely on his side.

"Let's move," I ordered, and my brothers nodded, their faces set in hard lines.

This wasn't over. Not by a long shot.

Chapter Sixteen
Eliza

Consciousness clawed its way back to me, dragging me through a thick haze of pain. My eyelids were leaden, resisting the urge to flutter open. When they did, darkness greeted me, thick and suffocating. I blinked, trying to orient myself, but the void clung stubbornly to my vision.

Lying there, my body felt like it had been trampled by a herd of elephants. Every breath was a battle, air scraping raw against my throat. The floor beneath me was cold, unforgiving concrete, and the stench of stale cigarette smoke and mildew assaulted my senses. Fear twisted in my gut and panic filled me as I tried to remember.

Bits and pieces shattered through the fog in my brain. The clubhouse. Jo's face, pale as death, eyes wide with terror. My father's gravelly voice slicing through the chaos, his silhouette looming over her. Two of his goons flanking him. I couldn't remember how they'd gotten in.

My head pounded and I pressed a hand to my forehead, closing my eyes as I struggled to piece everything together. More of what happened filtered through my thoughts.

"Stay still," one of them sneered at Jo, pressing a knife against her side. Seeing her so helpless against them infuriated me, and yet I was powerless against them.

"Eliza, come now," my father commanded, as if I were nothing more than a dog he could order around. "Or she gets it. Won't make me lose sleep to gut the little bitch."

I moved toward him, knowing if I didn't go, Jo could die. Her gaze followed me, brimming with tears. If my father hurt her, if that man so much as jostled her wrong or ended up stabbing her, then her baby could die.

I clenched my hands into fists, my nails biting into my palms. Jo needed me to be strong right now. I was the only one who could get her away from my father and his men. Even if it meant going back to the hell I'd barely survived before. For her, for the baby, I'd have to face it all.

"Cheshire," I whispered into the blackness, "where are you?"

I didn't know how much time passed, but I slipped in and out of consciousness. Pain clawed at me. My eyelids felt like sandpaper as they scraped open, revealing a sliver of dim light that stung. I blinked rapidly, but each throb pulsed a stark reminder -- I was alive.

More memories came to me.

"Eliza, we'll get you back, darlin'. You'll be home soon," Hatter said. I grabbed hold of his promise like a lifeline, needing something to cling to, some spark of hope.

"Keep Jo safe," I said, "and tell Cheshire..."

He shook his head. "You'll tell him yourself."

Before I could answer him, white-hot agony splintered across my skull, and the world went dark.

Now, the room swam into focus, more clearly this time. Grimy walls closed in on me, and the air was thick with must and fear. I wasn't alone. A few men huddled in the corner, their voices low, gruff -- predators just waiting to sink their teeth into prey.

But my father... he was absent. Where was he? What twisted game was he playing now?

"Hey, she's awake." One of them nodded in my direction. Their stares felt like bugs crawling over me.

I sucked in a shallow breath, bracing for what came next. Father's goons, no doubt. But why wasn't he here to gloat? What kind of hell had he left me in? Were they going to hurt me in his place?

"Boss has plans for you," another said, chuckling darkly. My stomach churned. Plans. Always plans. Like chess pieces, we were moved on his sick board.

"Shut it," a third snapped. "You're scaring her."

"Good," the first retorted with a sneer. "She should be scared."

Their laughter echoed in my ears. They were enjoying this, wanted me to suffer. Well, maybe not the one who'd tried to make them stop. Still, if he was working with my father, then he wasn't a good man.

The men's eyes were like daggers, sharp and cold, as they stared at me. They were my father's most trusted dogs. The fear crept up like a living thing inside me.

"Pretty little Eliza, all grown up and still so fragile," one of them sneered. His words felt like a knife twisting in my gut. Despair grabbed hold in a relentless grip. I was in deep, maybe too deep to ever claw my way out. If Cheshire didn't find me soon, I had a bad feeling he never would.

The fact my dad had brought me here -- wherever *here* was -- and not to the house, didn't bode well for my future.

My mind raced, my heart pounding a desperate rhythm. Cheshire. Would he find me? Could he?

He had to. The thought of never seeing those piercing blue eyes again, never hearing that smooth, confident voice laced with humor… No, I couldn't bear it.

I curled in on myself, arms wrapped tight around my middle. Vulnerable. So damn vulnerable. But I still had hope. Cheshire wouldn't let this be our end. Once he knew I'd been taken, he'd do anything to get me back. I didn't doubt him for a moment.

"Cheshire's not coming for you," one taunted, as

if reading my thoughts like an open book. "You're ours now."

But they didn't know Cheshire. Cunning, sly, always several steps ahead. He had to come. He just had to.

"Please," I whispered into the darkness, a plea to anyone listening. "Please…"

More time passed, the minutes dragging by slowly. I had no idea what time it was, or how long I'd been unconscious. Was it still the same day? Had Cheshire already found out I wasn't at the clubhouse anymore?

"Pathetic." The word cut through the silence. "Little bitch can't even sit up straight."

The mocking tone was a slap to the face. I glared at the shadowy figures, hate slowly burning through my fear. They were right. I couldn't save myself -- not now. But I swore on everything holy, if I got out I wouldn't be weak again. Never again. I'd do whatever it took to learn how to protect myself.

"Sheriff's got plans for you, Eliza," another voice chimed in, cruel delight in his tone. "A real nice future lined up."

Laughter echoed off the walls, chilling and heartless. My stomach twisted, bile rising hot and bitter in my throat. Yeah, I'd just bet he did.

"Someone's coming for you tomorrow," the first continued, coming to stand in front of me. "Man's looking for a delicate thing. Obedient."

"Little more than a slave," the second said, his words a dark promise. "And he paid a pretty penny for you."

The room seemed to spin. A slave. Property. If Cheshire didn't find me by tomorrow, my life would be over. This was hell. Just the thought of being helpless and owned by some unknown man filled me with dread. I'd rather die.

I bit back a sob, fists clenching till knuckles turned white. Fear clawed at me.

"Please," I murmured, not to them, but to the part of me that still held onto hope. "Don't let it end this way."

I closed my eyes, picturing Cheshire's smiling face. Right now, it brought me solace. But if this all went wrong, it would only serve as a reminder of everything I'd lost. I'd been too cautious, too afraid to dive deep into the heat between us. Now regret gnawed at me with sharp teeth. We could have shared so many more things together, if I hadn't been so hesitant.

The image of Cheshire's mischievous grin, those piercing blue eyes that saw through all my defenses, haunted me. If I had known our first time would be our last, I would have savored every second, let the day stretch into infinity.

A sudden crash jolted me from my thoughts. My pulse spiked, and I strained to hear over the *thump* of my own blood. Boots thundered outside, voices raised. The unmistakable clash of a fight.

"Cheshire?" The word was barely a breath, hope a fragile thing blooming in my chest.

Another bang, closer now. Shouts morphed into roars, feral and raw. Underland MC -- they had to be here. They *had* to be. My fingers curled into fists, knuckles scraping the cold floor as I willed the club to win, to be my salvation.

"Come on, come on," I murmured.

Fear warred with hope. Each punch thrown outside might bring rescue or seal my fate. But the thought of Cheshire storming through the door kept the darkness at bay.

"Please be him," I begged, desperate for the sight of that grin and the safety it promised. "Please, let this not be the end."

The noise swelled, and with it, a chance. My chance. If not for rescue, then at least for revenge. I steadied my breath, ready to fight, to claw my way back to him, back to us. I was starting to wish I'd had a chance to actually learn something from Carpenter. He'd been tasked with teaching me and Jo self-defense, but I'd been so battered, I hadn't been able to do much without hurting myself. Now I wished I'd pushed through the pain.

"Damnit!" One of the men stood, his chair scraping against the floor. "Come on. I think we need to get out there."

"What about her?" another one asked.

The first one snorted. "Does it look like she's fucking going anywhere? As long as we take down anyone trying to get into this room, she won't be leaving anytime soon."

All of them filed out, and I hoped the club managed to fight their way through them. I believed in Cheshire and the others. I had to. If they lost, then... it would all be over. I'd no longer have a reason to keep living, and I wasn't sure I'd want to. Not considering my father's plans for me.

* * *

Cheshire
A Few Hours Earlier

The moment we rolled up to the clubhouse, something felt off. The clubhouse door hung crooked on its hinges like a busted jaw. I killed the engine, my heart slamming in my chest.

"Shit," Knave muttered.

We were off our bikes in seconds, boots hitting the pavement hard. Mock and Rabbit flanked me, eyes wide. What the hell happened while we were gone?

Inside, the place was trashed. Chairs overturned, glass shattered. My gaze locked on Jo, curled up by Hatter's feet, her sobs breaking my damn heart.

"Eliza?" My voice was sharp, a blade cutting the air. I scanned the area, searching for her.

Hatter looked up. Jesus. What the hell happened to him? His eye was already turning black, and someone had busted his lip. As I looked around, I realized he wasn't the only one looking like they'd lost a fight.

"Holmes came here. Took Eliza."

"Fuck." My heart felt like it might break through my damn chest. I thought I'd been smart. Gone off to face Holmes and keep Eliza safe. Instead, I'd given him the opening he'd been waiting for. Had he lured us there on purpose?

"Used Jo as leverage." Hatter's hand was on Jo's shoulder, steady despite the quake in his voice.

"That explains your face. I'm guessing you didn't just stand back and let it happen."

Hatter shrugged. "Fighting didn't seem to do any good. Eliza went with him. To keep Jo safe. Damn sorry, Cheshire."

"Sorry doesn't cut it." My words were like ice. "We're getting her back."

"Whatever it takes," Hatter vowed. "We owe her a lot."

I stared at the mess in the clubhouse and felt the lack of warmth now that Eliza was gone. Rage erupted like a beast clawing out of my chest. I roared, the sound tearing from my throat as my fist shot out, coming down on the nearest table. Wood splintered under the force, a *crack* echoing through the clubhouse. My hand throbbed, but it was nothing compared to the fear gnawing at my gut.

Holmes could kill her. That thought hammered in my skull with each ragged breath. Eliza was caught in his twisted game. My fists clenched.

"Cheshire..." Jo's voice, small and wrecked, broke through the red haze.

I turned, and there she was. Her eyes filled with terror and pain. But alive. She took a hesitant step toward me, her arms open, seeking solace or maybe giving it.

"None of this is on you," I said as I pulled her into an embrace, feeling her tremble. "Glad you're safe. Eliza did what she had to do. I just wish like hell I'd realized what Holmes was up to and stopped it from happening."

She clung to me, her grip saying what words couldn't. Over the top of her head, my eyes locked with Hatter's. No need for words between us either. He saw the storm in my gaze.

I'm bringing her back. No matter what it takes.

The phone in my pocket vibrated. I pulled it out, Absolem's name flashing on the screen. What the fuck? Wasn't he here? Now that I thought about it, I hadn't seen him.

"Talk to me," I said when I accepted the call.

"Got something," Absolem's voice was steady, but I caught the undercurrent of urgency. "Wasn't easy. Had to pull strings, twist arms. Come to my room."

I hung up and walked quickly down the hall to Absolem's door. It was already open, and I stepped inside. He sat at his table with his laptop out, and a bunch of paper strewn everywhere.

"Location, Red," I said, using his given name. "Give it to me straight."

"Remember the warehouse you went to? He's at another one. Opposite side of town. Actually, outside of the town limits. It's heavily guarded. From what camera footage I could access, it looks like Holmes' boys are crawling all over it." I glanced over the papers on his table, trying to piece everything together.

"Risks?" I asked, though I already knew. When I went after Eliza, I'd be putting my life on the line.

"Big. It's tight there. But we can do it."

"Underland doesn't back down. And Eliza is one of our own now. We're getting her back."

Absolem followed me to the main room. We filled in Hatter and the others, and everyone agreed we had to go after Eliza. Hatter handed Jo off to Mock. He helped us prepare everything we'd need as the clubhouse became a hive of activity. Brothers loading guns with methodical precision, strapping knives to their belts or thighs. Hatter's gaze met mine -- grim and resolute.

"We're going to war for one of our own." I looked around the room at my brothers, knowing I could count on them.

Mock tossed me a shotgun, his face grim. "We got your back, Cheshire."

"Make sure you come back with her," Hatter added, his usual calm shattered by the sharp edge of concern.

"Nothing's stopping us. Tonight, Eliza comes home. Or we don't come back at all."

Knave checked his pistols, the clicks joining the symphony of preparation. Rabbit slipped a knife into his boot. My brothers, ready to ride into hell with me.

"It's time to bring her home."

The night air bit at my skin as our bikes growled to life. We filed out of the compound in a single line, our headlights cutting through the darkness as we rode through the streets, shadows slipping past sleeping houses, the only sounds the low rumble of our engines. My heart hammered against my chest, each beat a drum rallying me to fight, to save her. I heard an engine coming up behind us and glanced over my shoulder, seeing Hatter approach. I gave him a nod as he pulled up next to me. It looked like Jo had convinced him to join us.

The warehouse loomed ahead, ominous and still. Too quiet. I killed the engine, the sudden silence screaming in my ears. We dismounted, moving together. Absolem had said this place was heavily guarded, so where was everyone?

"Perimeter," I whispered. March nodded and slipped away, his frame melting into the shadows.

I felt it then -- the coil of tension before the storm, the edge of something deadly. It was more than just dark. It was the abyss staring back, hungry and cold. We were on its doorstep.

"Cheshire," Hatter's voice came low and urgent. "Time."

"Right." My fingers tightened on the grip of my gun. It was now or never. "Knave, you're with me. Rabbit, flank left. Mock, keep watch."

"Got it," they murmured, positions taken.

Eliza, I'm coming for you. Just hold on a little longer.

"Move in. Quiet," I said, but my gut screamed for speed, for action. My body thrummed with the need to burst through the door, to tear down anything between me and Eliza.

We crept closer, the building a hulking beast in

the moonlight. Then, the world exploded.

"Go, go, go!" I shouted as gunfire erupted. Bullets spat from the darkness. I saw the flash of a muzzle and returned fire.

"Cover!" Knave roared, his voice a battle cry.

"Cheshire!" It was Mock's voice, a warning.

I turned, a figure charging at me, knife glinting. No time to think. My arm shot out and I fired. He dropped with a *thud* on the ground.

"Push forward!" Hatter commanded, his presence a steady force amid the chaos.

"Clear!" Rabbit's voice cut through the din.

"Second floor," I yelled, taking the stairs two at a time, the others hot on my heels.

We reached the top and paused at the door, heart pounding, my gun ready. This was it, the moment of truth. I kicked the door open, my brothers at my back, ready to face hell itself.

"Eliza, wait for me. We're coming!"

The battle had begun in truth, and I wasn't walking out of here without my woman.

Chapter Seventeen

Cheshire

Holmes was close now. I could feel him. My blood hummed with the promise of the clash, every bruise and drop of sweat bringing me closer to the bastard who thought he could take what was mine. My brothers fought beside me, just as they always had.

"Cheshire!" The call ripped through space. "I'd thought for sure you'd die before you got this far."

"Here I come, Sheriff," I growled under my breath, my grin sharp, teeth flashing.

This was it. The final battle. And I wouldn't let him slip away again.

The air crackled with tension, thick enough to choke on. There he stood, Sheriff Holmes, his stance wide and the glint of madness in his eyes. I stepped closer, boots scraping against the debris.

We squared off, two predators circling. The room faded away, leaving just him and me locked in a silent war of wills. I knew his type -- no rules, no honor. Just raw, desperate power. My muscles tensed, ready for whatever dirty trick he'd pull. Men like him never fought fair.

Then, like a viper, he struck -- a wild haymaker swing aimed at my head. I could almost feel the *whoosh* of air as I ducked low, the punch missing by a hairsbreadth. Adrenaline surged through me, hot and electric, as I danced back.

"Nice try," I sneered. "You'll have to do better than that."

Holmes' face twisted into a snarl, and I braced myself. However long this took, I knew one thing for certain. Only one of us was walking out of here alive.

Holmes recoiled from his miss, and I saw my in.

No time for fancy moves -- this was street fighting, dirty and quick. I jabbed at his gut, his ribs -- anywhere soft, trying to do the most damage as quickly as possible. Each *thud* of knuckle against flesh was a promise, a silent vow that I'd end this.

"Ugh!" he grunted as I worked him over, relishing the sharp exhale of his pained breaths. His arms flailed, trying to guard his battered body, but I kept slipping through every crack in his defense.

"Is that all you got, Sheriff?" I taunted.

But pride's a dangerous thing. It blinds. And Holmes' booted foot came out of nowhere. It caught me square in the chest, the impact stealing my breath and sending me flying. Wood splintered as I crashed into some crates. The sound echoed throughout the room.

Pain exploded in my back, a thousand needles of wood piercing skin and muscle. Dust clouds rose around me. The air was thick with the scent of rot and old wood. I gasped, coughing, and feeling so much pain, I knew I'd have a deep and dark bruise later. But I couldn't stay down, not with Eliza's life on the line, not with victory so damn close.

"Come on, Cheshire," I muttered to myself, pushing through the pain. "Show this bastard what happens when you corner a cat."

I rolled to my side, spitting out the grit that had lodged in my mouth. My vision swam as I pushed up on shaky arms, every muscle screaming in protest. There was no time for pain, no space for weakness. Not here, not now.

Using the debris for leverage, I managed to haul myself upright. My fingers brushed against cold metal -- a pipe, abandoned and perfect. Grasping it like a lifeline, I surged to my feet, the weight of it oddly comforting in my grip.

Holmes was already stalking toward me. He didn't expect the arc of steel that whistled through the air toward him. With reflexes honed by dirty dealings and darker nights, he threw up an arm. The pipe met his forearm with a sickening *crunch*. For a second, pain flickered across his face.

"Didn't see that coming, did you?" I snarled.

He grunted, shaking off the hit like it was nothing. But I saw the wince, the slight falter. It was enough.

We clashed again, bodies colliding. His fist skimmed my jaw -- too close. I countered with a hook to his ribs that made him stagger back. I felt something give beneath my knuckles, and a twisted part of me smirked.

"Nice try, boy," Holmes spat, wiping blood from his lip.

"Boy?" I echoed, a laugh ripping from my throat. "That all you got, old man?"

Our dance was brutal, each step a strike meant to break bones or wills -- whichever gave out first. I ducked a wild swing, coming back with an uppercut. He blocked, then launched a kick aimed at my knee. I sidestepped, but the move cost me. Pain shot up my leg, a sharp reminder of the impact with those damned crates.

"Can't keep up?" Holmes ground out, reading my stumble all wrong.

"Keep dreaming," I threw back, teeth gritted.

This was survival, raw and unfiltered. Each hit was a testament to the hatred that had been brewing. Every punch I landed chipped away at the monster before me, a monster draped in the garb of a lawman.

I could feel the tide turning, each exchange of

violence bringing me closer to ending this nightmare. Eliza's face flashed before my eyes with every strike, her silent plea fueling my resolve. I wouldn't -- I couldn't -- let her down.

Not tonight. Not ever.

My lungs were burning, every breath a ragged drag. Sweat stung my eyes, but I couldn't afford to blink. Not with Holmes in front of me, every line of his body screaming murder.

"Getting tired, Cheshire?" His voice was a gravelly sneer as he circled me like a vulture.

"Something like that." My legs felt like jelly. Despite my exhaustion, I could keep going. But I had to make him believe he was winning.

Holmes' lips twisted into a cruel smile, and he lunged, fist barreling toward my face. It was now or never.

I dodged -- barely -- a whisper away from disaster. My adrenaline surged. Time slowed down, just enough. I pivoted, coiling power up from my toes, and let loose an uppercut that had every ounce of my strength behind it.

It connected. The *crunch* was sickeningly sweet.

Holmes' body crumpled, hitting the ground with a *thud* that echoed off the walls. Dust billowed around him.

My chest heaved as I watched him. But the bastard wouldn't stay down. Blood was smeared across his face, mixing with the dirt on the floor, yet he pushed himself up. His eyes locked onto mine, wild and unhinged.

"You... you won't win," he snarled, staggering to his feet, coming at me again.

"Keep telling yourself that," I shot back, readying for another round. I could have ended this easily. One shot to the head, but I felt like I needed to give him as much as he'd given Eliza over the years. A quick, clean death was too good for the likes of him.

Holmes lunged like a rabid dog, all froth and fury. I sidestepped.

"Come on, you son of a bitch," I said under my breath.

He came at me again, fists swinging wild. I ducked, felt the *whoosh* of air as his punch missed by an inch. Then I struck. Left jab to the gut. Right hook to the ribs. His breath hitched, his body buckling.

"This." *Crack*. My knuckles met his ribs again. "Is." *Crack*. My fist smashed into his face. "For." Another hit to his abdomen. "Eliza!"

I let loose with a barrage of punches, not letting up until I thought I might drop.

Holmes staggered, but his eyes still burned with that same damn madness. He spat blood, his grin a crimson smear. How the fuck was this asshole still standing?

"Fight's just starting, old man," I taunted, although, I had to admit I was slowing down.

I hit him again and again. Landing blow after blow.

"Is that all you've got?" His breath came out in a wheeze.

"More than enough for you," I shot back.

I watched him sway, read the defeat in his posture. Now. This was it. One last move.

With everything I had left, I punched, my fist connecting with his nose in a sickening *crack*. The sheriff's head snapped back, a spray of spit and blood painting the walls and floor.

Holmes hit the ground hard, a sack of meat and bone. He didn't get up. Not this time. His chest rose and fell -- too slow, too shallow -- but he was out. Finally.

I stood over him, breath ragged, heart slamming against ribs. It was done. For Eliza. For all those he'd harmed. The bastard wouldn't be terrorizing anyone else.

"Cheshire wins!" I panted, barely able to remain standing, but I'd managed to take the asshole down. Now I needed to make sure he stayed down.

Taking out my gun, I put two rounds in his chest and one between his eyes. There was no way he was coming back from that.

The silence that followed was heavy. It bore down on me. I turned away from the wreck of a man at my feet, and knew it was time to get Eliza.

Blood -- mine or his, I couldn't tell -- dripped from my knuckles. The room spun in a dizzying haze of adrenaline and pain.

"Cheshire…" Eliza? I turned to her, my legs shaky as a newborn foal. She rushed toward me, her eyes wide pools of fear and relief.

"Eliza," I managed, my voice barely above a grunt as I tried to catch my breath.

She reached out, her hands trembling as they touched my sweat-soaked skin. Grim satisfaction curled in my gut. We were alive. We'd won.

"Thank you," she whispered, her gaze scanning the cuts and bruises that painted my face and every inch of exposed skin.

"Anything for you," I said, meaning every damn word.

I yanked Eliza close, my arms a cage around her slight frame. Her body melded into mine, a perfect fit against all the broken pieces.

"Safe," I murmured into her hair, a promise

scrawled in sweat and blood. "You're safe now."

"Charlie…"

"Shh, I've got you." I felt her tears soak my shirt. I should have protected her better. Made sure her father could never touch her. I may have failed before, but this time I'd made certain he'd never hurt anyone ever again.

The world shrank down to the space we occupied, her and me, wrapped tight in the aftermath. Dust motes danced in the air, twirling in the dim light filtering through shattered windows.

"Cheshire." She clung to me, repeating my name as if it were some sort of prayer.

"Eliza, it's over." Her fingers clutched at my cut. "Love you more than anything. I would go to war for you anytime, anyplace."

"Love you too, Charlie. So much." Her grip tightened, as if she worried I'd disappear if she let go.

We swayed together, a silent dance in the ruins. Our breaths mingled, and the relentless beat of my heart slowed, matching hers. I finally had her back in my arms, right where she belonged. And I'd be damned if I'd let anyone take her from me again.

I peeled myself away from Eliza, the cold air biting at the sweat on my brow.

Hatter's boots crunched against debris. "Cheshire," he said, his voice low. "We need to move. I hear sirens heading this way. We've already freed the other women and girls."

"Right." I took Eliza's hand and led her through the wreckage and bodies.

March was already by the door. Rabbit and Carpenter flanked him, their faces set in grim lines. They all bore the marks of the night, bruises blooming like dark flowers against their skin.

"Let's clear out," March said, his words curt and clipped.

The weight of what had happened pressed down on us. Blood pooled on the floor, sticky underfoot. I wasn't sure how we were going to keep this from coming back to bite us on the ass.

"Come on," I said, tugging her along. The others moved ahead, shapes melting into the shadows.

"Where to?" she whispered.

"Anywhere but here," I replied.

"Okay." The simple word carried the weight of trust. She didn't need a location as long as she was with me.

Our story wasn't over, just paused on the precipice of a new chapter, ink about to spill across a fresh page. We'd survived the fight with her father, but we still had to take down the mayor and Robert Lewis before the entire fiasco would be over and done. But we'd taken a huge step tonight.

I helped Eliza onto my bike, and with Hatter taking the lead, we made our way back home.

Chapter Eighteen
Eliza

I took a deep breath, the kind you take when the world's weight finally lifts from your shoulders. Relief crashed over me like a tidal wave, and tears sprang to my eyes. I didn't bother trying to hold them back. Sheriff Holmes, my father, that monster in a badge, was nothing but ash and memories now. His empire lay in ruins at my feet.

My hands shook, not with fear this time, but with a freedom so fierce it burned through my veins. I laughed, the sound strange and foreign to my own ears. Free.

The clubhouse door swung open, and I stepped into chaos. It looked like Jo was prepping the place for a party. I noticed Park was with her.

He rushed over, coming to a stop a few feet away when Cheshire came in behind me, placing a hand on my shoulder.

"Eliza, I'm glad you're okay." Park cleared his throat. "Sorry about your dad. All things considered, he was still your flesh and blood, and the only family you had left."

I shook my head. "I'm not. I don't think anyone will miss him, except the men who were just as corrupt as him."

"Just the same… if you ever need someone to talk to…"

Cheshire growled and put himself between us. "She won't. Don't cross the line, Park!"

He lifted his hands and backed up. "Just being a friend. I figured she could use one. I think it's clear she's yours."

I placed my hand on Cheshire's back. "I'm fine.

He didn't mean anything by it. I'm going to get cleaned up."

"Same." Cheshire turned and leaned in closer, then lowered his voice so only I'd hear him. "Want to shower together?"

"Aren't you hurting? You look like one big bruise, not to mention the cut on your arm."

He cupped my cheek. "No amount of pain would ever stop me from enjoying your touch."

"Then, yes. I'd like that." He took my hand and led me through the room and down the hall. We stopped at my room long enough for me to grab a change of clothes.

"You'll need to move all your stuff later." He kissed my cheek. "My room is now *our* room. Unless you'd prefer to have a separate one."

I shook my head. "No. I like the idea of sharing one."

When we got to Cheshire's room -- no, *our* room -- he shut and locked the door. I set my clean clothes on the bed and went into the bathroom to start the shower. Cheshire joined me a moment later, already stripped out of his clothes. I winced when I saw all the cuts and bruises. I hadn't realized he had a cut other than the one on his arm.

"Doesn't it hurt?" I asked.

"Pain is a relative thing," he said. "And right now, I'm not letting it take me down. But later… yeah, it's going to hurt like a bitch and I'll be in agony."

I undressed and took his hand, tugging him into the shower. Using gentle strokes, I washed the grime from his skin, being extra careful around the open wounds. Even his lip had been split.

His touch was light as he traced the bruises on my body. "Aren't you in pain?"

"I'll be fine. I've had much worse," I said.

"That's not exactly comforting," he muttered.

"If you're trying to tell me not to touch you, and not to take this any further, then save your breath. I think we both need this right now. After everything, I want to feel close to you, and I want to celebrate the fact we're alive."

By the time I finished, he took the soap from me and washed the dirt from my skin. My nipples hardened from his light touch, and my body felt like it was on fire. No matter what he said, I worried I'd end up causing him pain if we were intimate right now. At the same time, I felt like I needed to be closer to him after everything we'd been through today.

"I want you, Eliza, but I don't think I'm in good enough shape to do this in the shower."

"Then let's dry off and move to the bedroom. We can be quick so we don't miss the party," I said.

He smiled a little. "The party will go most of the night. I don't think they'll mind us being a little late, but knowing Jo and my brothers, they've ordered food. I'm sure you're hungry."

Right on cue, my stomach rumbled and my cheeks flushed. He helped me out of the shower, and I noticed his arm was still bloody, as was as the cut on his side. Before he could drag me to the bedroom, I made him stand still and rummaged through his bathroom drawers and cabinet. I found some triple antibiotic and bandages. They wouldn't hold for long.

"I think you need stitches," I said.

"Later." He lifted me into his arms and carried me to the bed. He eased me down onto the mattress, pressing his body to mine. His eyes were filled with desire and ownership. "You're mine."

My heart raced at the thought of being owned by

him, completely under his control. With anyone else I'd be terrified. But I trusted Cheshire. Knew deep down that he'd never hurt me.

He kissed me, long and deep, as he trailed his hand down my thigh and slipped it between my legs. His fingers teased my pussy, and I arched my back, desperate for more. He slid a finger inside me, crooking it just right, and hit a spot inside me that had me begging for more.

My moans filled the room, and I couldn't help but wriggle beneath him in anticipation.

"Do you like that?" he asked, his voice low and devilish.

I nodded frantically, unable to form coherent words. He chuckled darkly and added another finger, stretching me until I was wet and ready for him.

Cheshire kissed me again before trailing kisses down my neck and collarbone. He positioned his cock against my pussy, and then stopped. "Tell me you want it," he said, his body hovering over mine.

"Please," I whimpered, begging for the pleasure he would give me. And then he thrust inside me, filling me up completely.

He started slowly, gradually increasing the pace as my body adjusted to his size. I cried out, loving the way he owned me completely. My hands gripped his shoulders, digging into his skin as I tried to hold on to the feeling.

"You're going to scream my name," he warned me. His pace quickened, and I could feel myself getting closer to the edge. I moaned his name as he thrust deeper, harder, hitting that sweet spot over and over again until my orgasm crashed down on me like a wave. I screamed his name, my body trembling from the intensity.

Cheshire thrust three more times, and I felt the heat of his release filling me. I briefly wondered if he'd forgotten the condom again by accident, or if he'd decided not to use one.

We lay there, panting heavily, our hearts still racing from the intense encounter. "That was... incredible."

He leaned in and nuzzled my neck. I couldn't help but agree. With each passing moment, I found myself falling deeper in love with him -- not just because of his brutal strength or his rugged good looks, but because he saw something in me that no one else had and accepted me completely, flaws and all.

We got up and rinsed off in the shower again. After I bandaged his wounds once more, we dressed and headed to the common room, straight into the belly of the celebration. Music pounded against the walls, a thumping bass that echoed the pulse racing under my skin. Laughter bubbled up around me, warm as the whiskey shots being tossed back.

"Eliza!" Hatter called out, his voice rough but laced with joy. He raised a bottle in salute. "To new beginnings! Your life is now your own."

"New beginnings," I echoed. Jo stood beside him, her delicate frame a stark contrast to the burly bikers surrounding her. Yet she radiated strength, her eyes fierce with a fire that refused to die. I hoped I could be like that one day.

We were survivors, both marked and molded by darkness, yet here we stood amidst laughter and light. She seemed to have adjusted well. Would I look so relaxed and carefree as more time passed?

The Underland MC had become an unexpected haven. I'd have never thought a place like this would be a sanctuary for me.

"Here's to tearing down tyrants," someone shouted, and the club erupted in agreement, a roar of approval that filled the space with electric energy. The club's work wasn't done, but by taking down my father, they'd taken a giant step in the right direction.

I weaved through the crowd, feeling more at home than I ever had before.

"You did good, Eliza," Mock said.

"I didn't do anything except wait."

"Couldn't have been easy," Carpenter said, clapping me on the back so hard I nearly stumbled.

"Thanks to you all, I had a reason to wait for someone to come rescue me," I said. "If something like that had happened before I met all of you, I would have just waited to die. But I knew Cheshire, and the rest of you, would keep looking for me."

Cheshire cut through the room, his presence turning heads, his perpetual grin promising mischief. The sea of bodies parted for him. He locked eyes with me from across the room, blue gaze blazing. Pride. Adoration. A silent vow that spoke louder than any words.

"Eliza," he called, his voice slicing through the clamor. Every step he took toward me was a claim, each stride a testament to his place in this world -- and in mine. When he reached me, the chatter and the din of celebration dulled into oblivion.

"Cheshire," I whispered, my heart hammering.

His fingers curled around mine, possessive yet gentle. He tugged, and I followed, drawn by an invisible thread that bound us. As he led me to the center of the room, it was clear who I belonged to, clear that I wasn't just part of the club -- I was part of him. My cheeks warmed, and I couldn't hold back my smile.

* * *

Cheshire

The thrum of the bass pulsed through the soles of my boots as I pulled Eliza into me. Our bodies found a rhythm, a primal dance older than time, her hips against mine. The room faded away, everything dimming against the electricity between us.

"Eliza," I murmured, voice low, my breath hot on her neck. She tilted her head, offering the expanse of skin where her pulse danced beneath. My arm wrapped tighter around her waist, pulling her closer until there was no space for doubt or fear -- only us, only this. I didn't care who was watching. Let them. Especially Park, that fucker. I wanted him to know Eliza was mine.

We spun, dancing to the music. It felt as if the world was spinning. Our feet moved to the beat, and I wanted the moment to last forever. I couldn't remember a time I'd ever enjoyed dancing with a woman like this.

I leaned in, slow, deliberate. Her breath hitched, anticipation crackling between us, fierce and feral. Then our lips met and the club erupted in applause and catcalls.

"Get it, Cheshire!" someone hollered, the shout piercing through the haze of heat wrapping us. I flipped off the room in the general direction of the voice and heard someone laugh.

Cheers, whistles, the clinking of bottles -- I knew it might have embarrassed any other woman. But not Eliza. Not my fierce lady who'd stared down hell with the steel of a warrior queen. She was far braver than she gave herself credit for.

Our kiss deepened, a clash of teeth and tongue. It wasn't gentle. It wasn't meant to be. It was fire and need, a claiming more powerful than any ink on skin. Her fingers dug into my shoulders, nails biting through leather and shirt, branding me as surely as I branded her with every press of my mouth.

We broke apart, breathless, chests heaving. Her cheeks were flushed, lips bruised from our fervor, but her eyes… they blazed with a light that outshone the stars in the sky.

"Mine," I growled, low enough for only her to hear.

"Yours," she said.

This party was about more than a victory. It was a beginning -- the first mile of a long ride into a future we'd carve out together. When we were done, this town would be safe. No more monsters would lurk in the shadows. If they dared come to Warren, we'd take them down.

* * *

Eliza

The noise died down, glasses lifted high as Hatter commandeered the silence.

"Brothers," he began, his gaze sweeping over the sea of leather and ink. "And, sister. Tonight, we aren't just celebrating a win. It's another step toward a much bigger plan."

"Eliza," Hatter continued, his eyes finding mine in the crowd. "You've shown more spine than anyone ever gave you credit for."

I swallowed hard, the lump in my throat a mix of pride and raw emotion. Around us, the noise rose to a crescendo again, a wave of cheers and hoots.

"Here's to new beginnings," Hatter roared over the din, "to the end of tyranny in Warren, and to the Underland MC -- may our roads be long and our enemies scatter like dust!"

"Underland!" the club echoed back.

Conversations sparked around me, tales of close calls and daring plans. I let their words wash over me.

"Can't believe we pulled it off," someone said. "And we didn't lose anyone."

"Believe it, brother," another replied, and I heard the sound of someone slapping another person on the back. "We're damn unstoppable."

They laughed, and the sound was pure joy, a release of all the darkness we'd been buried under.

"Feels like waking up," I murmured to myself, watching the scene unfold.

"Damn good morning, then." Cheshire's voice rumbled next to me, his arm snaking around my waist. "We earned every second of this, Eliza. You especially."

I leaned into him, the beat of his heart soothing me. We were battered, maybe a little broken, but we were here, together.

"Need air," I murmured to Cheshire, breathless from the crush of bodies.

"Follow me," he said, gripping my hand.

We slipped through the front door and into the cool night. Quiet wrapped around us. The sound of the club celebrating could still be heard through the walls of the clubhouse, but out here, it was just us in the moonlight.

"Scared you today, didn't I?" he asked, his thumb tracing the line of my jaw.

"Scared *for* you," I corrected him. I reached out to run my fingers over his cut. The patches told stories, even if I didn't know what they were.

"I'm never going to leave you," he vowed, pulling me close. "I'll be by your side always."

"Promise?" My voice cracked on the word, hope and fear tangling together.

"Promise, Eliza." He sealed it with a kiss that tasted like forever.

"Love you," I breathed against his lips, the truth of it simple and raw.

"Love you more," he answered, his grin the last thing I saw before closing my eyes and leaning into him.

After Cheshire kissed me breathless, we returned to the clubhouse. The music died down, and the chatter settled into a low hum. All eyes turned to Hatter as he stood. Jo was beside him, her hand on his arm, looking like she was holding onto the world.

"Got something to say." Hatter's voice rumbled through the room, commanding silence.

My heart kicked against my ribs. Something big. I could feel it in the way Cheshire tensed next to me, his fingers tightening around mine. Were they about to tell everyone about the baby? The way Jo's face glowed said it was something that involved them both.

"Jo's pregnant."

A cheer exploded from the club members, raw and joyous.

"Congrats, brother!" someone yelled over the din.

"Family's growing," another voice followed.

I watched as they swarmed Hatter and Jo, a sea of leather and ink. They were more than a club. They were kin, bound by something stronger than blood. And Jo, with her wide smile and eyes shining, was the queen of it all.

"Damn good news," Cheshire murmured, squeezing my hand.

"Amazing," I agreed, my voice nearly lost in the

celebration.

Hatter's scarred face was split by a grin. It was the first time I'd seen him that happy since I'd come to the clubhouse.

"New life," Cheshire said, his gaze not leaving the pair at the center of the room. "Means we're doin' something right. That the club has a future."

I leaned up to whisper to him. "Did you forget something earlier on purpose? Are you wanting a family too?"

He tensed and stared at me. "Shit. Sorry, Eliza. Maybe some part of me did it on purpose, but I'd promised to give you the choice and I fucked it up again."

I shook my head. "No. Like I told you before, if we have a baby, then it was meant to happen. I'm not scared anymore. I have you, and everyone else here."

Cheshire held my hand, his grip tight, as if he was afraid to let go. I didn't mind.

"Look at them," I whispered, nodding toward Hatter and Jo. "They're so happy."

"Deserve it," Cheshire replied, his voice rough with emotion.

"Yeah, they do."

"Like us," he added, turning to look at me.

"Like us," I echoed.

The darkness that had clung to our lives was receding, pushed back by the light of new beginnings. When I looked up at Chesire, I saw a man who'd walked through hell with me, who'd fought for a peace we could finally call our own.

"Ready for this?" he asked, his thumb stroking the back of my hand. "For a new life?"

"More than ready." I leaned my head against his shoulder.

Epilogue

Cheshire

I leaned against the frame of the kitchen doorway, arms crossed. Eliza and Jo were a whirlwind of motion in front of the stove. Jo's laugh, a rare sound, cut through the sizzle of the pan, and mingled with Eliza's lighter chuckles. It was a good sound. Honest. Real.

They tossed ingredients back and forth like they were born to it. The scent of spices hit the air, sharp and inviting. The whole place smelled like comfort, like something you could sink into and forget the rest of the world.

My gaze stuck to them, watching how they moved together. Eliza had this way about her -- graceful, like she danced through life. She'd relaxed so much over the past few weeks.

Jo's movements were always more careful, measured, but there was strength there.

I thought about the roads we'd all traveled to get to this point. It hadn't been an easy ride. My past -- a twisted road of mistakes and close calls. Eliza had lived a miserable existence thanks to her father. And Jo, she'd had it rougher than anyone should. But there they were, the two of them, finding some kind of peace while doing something as mundane as cooking.

The club had been my family, always would be. I would bleed for them. But this -- Eliza and Jo -- it felt different. The two of them were a breath of fresh air.

"Cheshire, are you going to stand there all day, or are you going to come help?" Eliza's voice snapped me back, her tone playful and happy.

"Thought I'd admire the view a bit longer," I shot back, a grin spreading across my lips.

Eliza spun around, her smile lighting up the kitchen. The look in her eyes made me feel like she had a secret just for me. Through the *clang* of pots, and their chatter, I watched her and admired her every move.

"Need a taste tester?" I asked, stepping closer.

"Always," she said. "But I'm still learning. Be thankful Jo is here to guide me."

I always had the answer, the next plan. But not this time. For once, it felt like I was standing on a precipice. Was I ready to jump?

She turned back to the stove, unaware of the storm she'd stirred in me. My hands itched to pull her close, to sink into that warmth and light she exuded. But there was more I had to do, a promise I needed to make real.

"Eliza," I started, then stopped. *Get your shit together, Charlie.* And yes, right now I was Charlie and not Cheshire.

"Cheshire?" She looked at me, head tilted, concern flickering in her eyes. "You good?"

"Yeah," I said, but my voice sounded rougher than I wanted it to be. "Better than good."

I'd been waiting for weeks, and now I knew this was it. The perfect time. No chaos from club business, no past ghosts howling at our backs. Just her and me in a kitchen that smelled like home.

"Eliza," I tried again, and this time my voice held steady. "There's something I've been wanting to --"

The words hung there, suspended between us. Her eyes locked on mine, and I could see it -- the question, possibly the beginning of understanding. Before I could say anything, she turned away.

Even though I no longer had her attention, I knew it had to be now or never.

"Eliza," I said, and I knew there was no going

back. "I've got something to ask you."

The weight burned a hole in my pocket. My fingers fumbled, wrapping around the small box that held every damn hope I had. Eliza's back was to me, as she hummed some tune I couldn't place, and stirred something that smelled like heaven. Either she hadn't heard me, or… No, it had to be that she hadn't heard me. I didn't think she'd ignore me.

"Cheshire?" Jo's voice sounded sharp. "You look like you're about to jump out of your skin."

I shot her a glare, telling her with my gaze to can it. I couldn't have her spooking Eliza. Not now.

"Nothing," I ground out. "Just thinking."

"Uh-huh." Jo wasn't buying it, but she stepped away, giving me room. Room to breathe. Room to dive into whatever the hell this could be.

My knees felt weak, which pissed me off because weakness hadn't been my style. But for Eliza? Hell, I would have crawled through broken glass.

"Eliza," I said, drawing her attention again.

She turned, all warmth and questions.

"Cheshire, what's --" Eliza started, but her words cut off when my knee hit the floor. Hard.

"Jesus, Cheshire!" Jo gasped, clapping a hand over her mouth. Her eyes were as wide as saucers, and I knew she'd figured it out.

My hand shook as I fished out the ring. I should have practiced this part. It was too late now. Eliza's gaze zeroed in on me. There was no backing out now, not with the way she was looking at me.

"Cheshire…" Eliza whispered.

"Eliza, you're so damn beautiful, it hurts to look at you sometimes."

The box's *creak* was loud in the silence. Jo's eyes were locked on it, one hand still muffling her gasp. The club might as well have been a church right then for all the reverence hanging in the air.

"Shit," I muttered under my breath, thumbing the lid open wider.

Inside, the ring caught the dim light. It was real, a band of white gold with a diamond that wasn't too flashy but was far from small.

"Damn, Cheshire..." Jo mumbled.

"Keep it down," I shot back, but there was no heat in it. My focus was all on Eliza, on the ring, on the jump my heart gave when our eyes met again. Her face lit up, like I just handed her the sun, moon, and stars.

"Want to try it on?" I asked.

She nodded and I took the ring from the box, sliding it onto her finger. My throat felt tight as I stared at it.

"Look at that," I said, more to myself than anyone else. "Fits you."

"Cheshire, it's..." She trailed off, but I saw it in her eyes. "Beautiful."

"Eliza, I'm not good with fancy speeches, and God knows I've been on the wrong side of many tracks." Her gaze locked onto mine, steady and expectant. The kitchen, with its bubbling pots and scents of garlic and oil, faded away until there was just her, just us. "Will you marry me?"

The words came out all twisted, raw around the edges. But they were honest. They were me, laid bare.

She didn't move for a heartbeat, two. Time was a damn traitor, stretching seconds into lifetimes. Then, those beautiful eyes of hers started to glisten, wet and bright. Her lips parted, no sound coming out yet, but everything was written there, clear as day.

"Charlie..." Her voice caught on my real name.

"Say yes, Eliza." It was half-plea, half-demand.

The rest of my life was dangling right there in her answer.

And then she nodded, quick and sure, a single tear tracking down her cheek. "Yes, Charlie. Yes."

Relief punched through me. I rose up, the weight of the world sliding off my shoulders. She'd said yes. To me, to this, to a forever that would be wild but so worth it.

Eliza's hand was still in mine, her ring catching the dim light. I pulled her close, my other arm wrapping around her waist. She fitted against me, perfect as if custom-made for me, her body warm and soft.

"Look at you," I murmured. "My fiancée."

"Your fiancée," she echoed back, her smile so damn bright it blinded me.

We were two pieces of a busted-up puzzle, finding our fit in a world that wasn't too kind on the best of days. But somehow, we'd found each other, and we were just right together.

"Cheshire, this is real, right?" Eliza asked.

"Damn right it is." The words came out gruff, like they were dragged up from somewhere deep inside.

Her eyes -- they were sparkling, little stars caught in a dark sky. I leaned in, my forehead against hers. "You and me, doll."

"Against the world." Her whisper was fierce, a promise wrapped up in two words.

"Always." I meant it. Been through hell and back, but this was different. This was choosing the hard road because there was sunshine waiting on the other side.

"Love you, Cheshire." The words spilled from her lips, raw and unguarded.

"Back at you, Eliza." It's all I had, but it was enough.

We stood there, soaking up the moment. The rest of the world could wait. Right then, it was just us -- the thumping of our hearts syncing up, ready to take on whatever came next. Together. Always together.

I hadn't been looking for her, but I'd managed to find one person in this entire world meant to be mine, and I was going to hold onto her with everything I had.

Harley Wylde

Harley Wylde is an accomplished author known for her captivating MC Romances. With an unwavering commitment to sensual storytelling, Wylde immerses her readers in an exciting world of fierce men and irresistible women. Her works exude passion, danger, and gritty realism, while still managing to end on a satisfying note each time.

When not crafting her tales, Wylde spends her time brainstorming new plotlines, indulging in a hot cup of Starbucks, or delving into a good book. She has a particular affinity for supernatural horror literature and movies. Visit Wylde's website to learn more about her works and upcoming events, and don't forget to sign up for her newsletter to receive exclusive discounts and other exciting perks.

Harley at Changeling: changelingpress.com/harley-wylde-a-196

Bad Boys Multiverse
Contemporary MC, Organized Crime, and Crossovers
A Bad Boy Romance
Dixie Reapers MC
Devil's Boneyard MC
Hades Abyss MC
Devil's Fury MC
Reckless Kings MC
Savage Raptors MC
Swift Angels MC
Owned by the Mob
Bryson Corners
Underland MC

Paranormal MC
Devoted Guardians MC
Balor's Saints MC

Print and Audio:
Dixie Reapers MC Print
Dixie Reapers MC Audio
Devil's Boneyard MC Audio
Hades Abyss MC Audio
Devil's Fury MC Audio

Changeling Press LLC

Contemporary Action Adventure, Sci-Fi, Steampunk, Dark Fantasy, Urban Fantasy, Paranormal, and BDSM Romance available in e-book, audio, and print format at ChangelingPress.com – MC Romance, Werewolves, Vampires, Dragons, Shapeshifters and Horror -- Tales from the edge of your imagination.

Where can I get Changeling Press Books?

Changeling Press e-books are available at ChangelingPress.com, Amazon, Apple Books, Barnes & Noble, Kobo, Smashwords, and other online retailers, including Everand and Kobo Subscription Services. Print books are available at Amazon, Barnes and Noble, and by ISBN special order through your local bookstores.

ChangelingPress.com